the BETTE DAVIS
MURDER CASE

the BETTE DAVIS

MURDER CASE

by GEORGE BAXT

ST. MARTIN'S PRESS   NEW YORK

Design by Basha Zapatka

Library of Congress Cataloging-in-Publication Data

Baxt, George.
    The Bette Davis murder case / George Baxt.
        p.   cm.
    ISBN 0-312-10939-3
    1. Christie, Agatha, 1890–1976—Fiction.   2. Davis, Bette, 1908–1989—Fiction.   3. Motion picture actors and actresses—England—London—Fiction.   4. Women authors, English—England—London—Fiction.   5. London (England)—Fiction.   I. Title.
    PS3552.A8478B47   1994
    813'.54—dc20   94-6590
                                                                     CIP

First Edition: August 1994
10 9 8 7 6 5 4 3 2 1

This Book Is for Two of My Favorite Ladies,
Ann Bayer and Patricia Johnston

1

VIRGIL WYNN'S BROW WAS DOTTED WITH beads of perspiration. He clutched his stomach as he sank onto a chair. His personal physician was baffled. Virgil had undergone a series of tests and examinations, but there seemed to be no explanation for his recurring abdominal pains, the loss of appetite, and the fainting spells. He stared at the small statue of the Egyptian queen Nefertiti. It rested on a pedestal under a portrait of the cruel pharoah Amenhotep. On the opposite wall there hung a rendering of another pharoah, Ramses II. The library was heavily populated with Egyptian artifacts. There were representations in one form or another of the deities Isis and Ptah and a number of lesser lights of the Egyptian heavens who for one reason or another hadn't made marks of greater importance as objects of worship. There was Nokus, presumed to be the god of basket weaving, and one of Virgil's favorites, Petera, whom Virgil had been told by an old soothsayer was the god of pederasts; but Virgil distrusted the information, as the soothsayer surrounded himself with a coterie of young boys. Ancient royalty was well represented by Queen Ramatah, who was reputed to have been a contortionist; young King Tut, unearthed only fourteen years before, in 1922; the fascinating King Ptolemy; and the inevitable royal cliché, Cleopatra.

The pain disappeared as rapidly as it had attacked, and Virgil mopped his brow with a handkerchief with which he also dried his sweaty palms. Why can't the bloody doctors come up with a proper diagnosis? he wondered for the fifth time that afternoon. When he had found the tomb of Queen Ramatah and eagerly supervised its opening, one of his Egyptian aides had warned him of the curse he'd be unleashing.

Virgil recalled the scene and how he had addressed young Rami Tup. "Curse? What curse? We British are impervious to curses. We don't put stock in them. We've accumulated these ephemeral curses in India, Africa, Mesopotamia, the West Indies, the East Indies, Egypt, and Northern Ireland. Now, start the digging."

Soon he'd be off on another expedition to Egypt, in the Valley of the Kings, for over a century a magnet for archeologists around the world. If only his damned stomach could be brought under control. This accursed stomach. Maybe it's true. My stomach is cursed. The Wynns had been celebrated for many centuries for their dicky stomachs, his father, Lord Roland Wynn, himself a celebrated archeologist, had told him.

His father. Lord Roland Wynn. Knighted in 1920 for his discovery of Queen Baramar's tomb. Virgil remembered how as a young man he had stood watching proudly as the king touched his father's shoulders lightly with a sword, dubbing him a knight. He hadn't heard the queen say under her breath, "The very idea of knighting a grave robber." Lord Roland's celebrity was short-lived. In 1922 he was eclipsed by the discovery of Tutankhamon's tomb by Howard Carter and Lord George Herbert Carnarvon. He remained in eclipse despite five years of feverishly digging around for any other ancient celebrity, only to be forced into near-obscurity by his own son Virgil.

Once he got going on the archeological scene, Virgil proved to be a whiz at nosing out the sites of hidden tombs. He was compared to the pigs that uncover truffles. Unlike his father,

Virgil became a very wealthy man, the envy of his two older siblings, Oscar, a self-styled composer, and Anthea, who wrote poetry, both surviving by Virgil's generosity, as also did Lord Roland. Virgil took a deep breath. His housekeeper, Nellie Mamby, materialized, carrying a tea tray.

"Oh, God, Mamby, have mercy. I couldn't possibly drink or eat anything."

She asked with concern, "Have you had another attack, sir?"

"Only a slight discomfort this time."

"The tea will do you good," she insisted as she set the tray on his desk and promptly poured him a cup.

He crossed to the desk and sat, watching the steam rising from the teacup. "Smells good."

"And it's strong." She was a small woman with a strong face dominated by a pair of gray eyes that pierced whatever object they brought into focus. They penetrated Virgil's handsome face as the forty-year-old man sipped the tea.

He grimaced. "Very strong, very hot."

"The way tea should be served," she said firmly. "Are you in for dinner?"

"Don't fuss. If I eat anything, it'll be some gruel or some consommé."

"I've got some lovely chops," she said enticingly.

"You eat them." He knew she would, and without being coaxed. Nellie Mamby had the voracious appetite of those who had suffered deprivation in their youth. In Virgil Wynn's kitchen, Nellie Mamby was an empress, the kitchen her private domain where few dared venture across the threshold, and even fewer desired to.

Virgil now stood in front of a bust of King Ptolemy. "Look at the bugger. The defiance. The arrogance. The mystery. A genius. He was an astronomer, a geographer, a mathematician. He believed that the earth was the center of the universe and the heavenly bodies moved around it." She'd heard the litany many times before, but like a good, well-trained servant, she patiently listened to it again. Virgil and his family never ceased to amaze and interest her. Father and son archeologists, snooping about in ancient tombs and disturbing the dead. She wondered if in some century in the future an archeologist might come across her burial place and mistakenly identify her as long-lost royalty. Anthea, the eldest, the poet, forever pleading with Virgil to pay her gambling debts. Oscar, the next in the pecking order, a composer who to her knowledge had never had anything performed either on the wireless or in a concert hall. Virgil was a good and a fair employer. He always smiled, always had a kind word, and seemingly enjoyed her mediocre cooking, possibly because he didn't know any better. Archeological expeditions were rarely celebrated for their cuisine.

Virgil droned on. "The Ptolemys were a Macedonian family, you know. . . ." Nellie refrained from saying, 'God, yes.' "They formed the ruling dynasty of Egypt from about 323 to 44 B.C."

"Seems like a nice long run, sir."

"Ptolemy the First reigned from about 323 to 284 B.C. He's the one I'm after this time." Javert on the scent of Jean Valjean. "And, by golly, I shall find him!"

Mamby wondered why some international missing-persons bureau hadn't been established for the sole purpose of locating lost Egyptian tombs. Maybe it was something Scotland Yard could look into and perhaps they could earn some profit. They were always complaining of lack of funds in these dreadful economic times.

Virgil was back sitting behind the desk. "Take away the tea things, Mamby. I must get back to work." He had barely touched his tea, just a few sips. But as she glided out of the room, he could feel the stomach pains returning and he slumped back in the chair, begging for mercy in a whisper and knowing none would be forthcoming.

* * *

The *Duchess of Bedford*, a small but proud liner, dipped and rose as it slowly cut a swath across the Atlantic Ocean towards Liverpool. Below-decks, in a first-class cabin, Harmon Nelson lay on his bed recovering from a fever he thought he had contracted when the ship made its way through the Panama Canal from the Pacific side to the Atlantic side, having embarked from a port in Vancouver. He watched his wife lighting a cigarette, then inhaling deeply and then exhaling ferociously. "Ham" (his nickname), "my mind's made up." She was pacing—short, jerking steps, arms flailing about in a mannerism familiar to movie audiences. "I want a divorce. Not this minute. Not today. Not tomorrow. Not next week. Not next month. But sooner or later, a divorce. It's no use kidding ourselves. We married much too young. Don't you agree?"

"Don't I always agree?" She could hear the fever in his voice.

"Oh, don't be tedious, darling. I'm looking forward to a life in exile even less then you are. But the move had to be made. You shouldn't have insisted on coming along."

"At the time I thought it was a husband's duty."

"Well, yes, of course, quite right. And my mother agreed with you, and since Ruthie agreed, I decided to let you come. But on this tedious voyage I've had too much time to think. London's going to be a long, tiresome, drawn-out affair. It may be months before I go to trial; at least that's what Sir William wrote me. Ham, you'll be miserable."

"I'm miserable now."

"You poor thing. I can hear how feverish you sound." She thought for a moment. "Good grief, I hope it's not something contagious, something fatal."

He said solemnly, "Marriage can often be contagious, and it can frequently be fatal."

She was mulling over what he had said. "Oh. I guess that's supposed to be funny."

"I'm never funny."

"I won't dispute that."

"Let's not have a fight."

"Absolutely not. We'll soon be in England. We must be civilized about the split the way the British would be, or are supposed to be." A hand flew to her forehead. "Oh, God! Why did I choose to run away to England? Why not France, where both the cuisine and the weather are better? I don't know a soul in England."

"You know George Arliss."

"Poor old dear. Did I tell you it was he who got Jack Warner to sign me to a contract?"

"Many times."

She ignored the remark. "Dear old George taught me so much about acting for the camera. He transformed me from a brown mouse into a blond glamour girl." Her face hardened. "Glamour! Ha! Paul Muni gets fifty thousand per picture. I get a measly sixteen hundred a week, and I stole *Bordertown* right from under his nose! Eddie Robinson gets forty thousand a picture. That old frump Ruth Chatterton gets eight thousand a week, and her pictures lose money! But me! Me! The winner of an Academy Award, which none of them has ever won! What do I get? A lousy sixteen hundred a week!"

Ham said slowly, "In the time of a great world depression, with Okies migrating from the Dust Bowl to California, with tent cities springing up in every city of the United States, with long lines forming at free soup kitchens, sixteen hundred a week sounds pretty good to me."

She rubbed the cigarette out in an ashtray as she exploded, "I knew it! I knew it all along! I suspected it from the way you always laugh at Jack Warner's embarrassing jokes!"

"I don't laugh at the jokes. I laugh at him."

"I knew it I knew it I knew it. You're on *his* side. You want me to lose my case!"

He kept calm. "Bette, this is 1936, not 1926, when everything was caviar and bootleg champagne. Come down to earth. Warner Brothers have been building your career very carefully."

"*What!*" She seemed to tower over the bed and its weary occupant as she clenched and unclenched her fists, a human volcano. "I had to fight and scream and threaten to get them to lend me to Radio Pictures for *Of Human Bondage*. I get nominated for an Oscar, but does Jack Warner care? Like hell he does. He tosses me into garbage like *The Girl from Tenth Avenue* and *Dangerous*."

"Well, you got your Oscar for that one!"

"Consolation prize!"

"Is there no satisfying you?"

"God damn it, I can never get through to you! The only time you seem to be receptive is when you're in front of your cheesy dance band waving your baton. You always look serene then!"

"That's because I'm listening to music, not to you."

"Why, you . . ." She was looking around for something to throw at him.

"There's a pillow on the easy chair," he pointed out affably.

She folded her arms and glared at him. "Harmon Oscar Nelson . . ."

". . . Junior . . ."

"I hope this God-damned disease of yours is fatal."

"Sweetheart, how often have you slept with George Brent?"

"Not often enough, you son of a bitch!" She grabbed a raincoat she had earlier slung across the back of a chair and made what she hoped was a very dramatic exit from the stateroom, slamming the door.

She paused to brush away the tears of anger and remorse that were welling up. She struggled into the raincoat and headed for an upper deck. Once outside she fumbled in the coat pockets hoping for a pack of cigarettes, but she was out of luck. She realized she had been swallowed up in a thick fog.

The ship's foghorn mourned dolefully as she walked to the rail and leaned on it. Bette suppressed a shudder and returned to dwelling on the future.

Bette Davis. Actress. Star under contract to the tyrants Warner. Actress. Damned good actress, despite all the odds against her. When six years earlier she'd been brought to Hollywood from Broadway, where she had drawn some attention to herself in Myron Flavin's play *Broken Dishes*, Carl Laemmle, Jr., scion of the mogul who ruled Universal pictures and who had signed Bette, commented nastily, "She's about as sexy as Slim Summerville." Summerville was a very tall, lanky actor with a basset-like face. Universal got rid of her fast, and she was relegated to Poverty Row quickies until George Arliss read her for the role opposite him in *The Man Who Played God*. He saw something in her few others recognized. He realized she was no carbon-copy ingenue; she was an original. She had style, a crisp, clipped way of delivering dialogue. She was refreshing. He convinced Jack Warner to sign her, and in just a few weeks the brown mouse was a blond leading lady with a big future.

Was she really? Was Ludovico Toeplitz really her future in England? The forty-five-year-old Italian producer had offered her fifty thousand dollars to star in *I'll Take the Low Road*, about an American heiress hoping to snare a royal husband in Europe. Ham had asked, "What makes you think this is an improvement on the scripts Jack Warner has lined up for you?"

The thought of his comment had her seething again. The pictures Jack had lined up for her. *Mountain Justice* and the role of an Ozark hillbilly accused of murder, or was it witchcraft? *God's Country and the Woman* as a woman lumberjack or something like it.

"Garbage! It's all garbage!" she shrieked into the fog.

"I can't see a bloody thing!" said a very well modulated female voice coming from her left.

"Oh," said Bette, "you startled me."

"I'm so sorry. I didn't mean to. But when you shrieked, 'Garbage! It's bloody garbage!' I thought you could see some flotsam and jetsam, and I was terribly envious." She was coming closer. "Out here I feel the lack of a walking stick, a tin cup, and a guide dog. There, now I can see you. Oh, of course, you're the movie actress. You were pointed out to me in the dining saloon. How's your husband? I hear he's been laid up since the Panama Canal."

"He's still laid up and he's a beast. Sorry. I shouldn't have said that. He's really quite nice if you like that sort of thing. You know who I am. I'm at a disadvantage."

She said smoothly, "I'm Nydia Tilson, and I'm wondering why I booked this bloody tub when I could have taken the train to New York and luxuriated on the *Bremen* or the *Normandie.*"

"I can understand how you feel, but I don't mind the *Duchess of Bedford* at all. I wanted a long sea voyage. It's my first . . . vacation in too many years." Nydia Tilson was lighting a cigarette. Bette sounded like Oliver Twist asking for seconds. "I don't suppose you have another cigarette you can spare?"

"Oh, dear, whatever has happened to my manners? That's what two weeks in Hollywood do to one." She held a lighter to Bette's cigarette. She'd never seen anyone inhale and exhale so ferociously. The actress might have been descended from dragons.

"I feel much better. Thank you so much."

"I say, now that we've begun a conversation, I very selfishly don't want to end it too soon. It's teatime. Can I interest you in a spot? They do a real, proper British tea."

"As opposed to a real improper British tea?"

"I couldn't get *any* kind in Hollywood." Bette followed Nydia Tilson into the ship's saloon, where several other passengers were already sipping tea and gorging on scones, cakes, and minute cucumber-and-butter sandwiches on black bread.

In the light of the saloon, Bette sized up her new acquaintance. The first thing that struck her was her gorgeous skin.

When Nydia removed the scarf around her head, Bette admired her beautifully coiffured hair. She wore a simple skirt and blouse, with a sweater hanging loosely from her shoulders. After ordering the tea and waiting for it to be served, they chitchatted about nothing of importance, finally getting onto the subject of London hotels.

Bette told her, "I'll be staying at the Savoy."

"Oh, very nice," commented Nydia. "It's on the Thames. Be sure to demand a room on the Thames side. The views are exquisite. The hotel adjoins one of our best restaurants, Simpson's on the Strand, the Savoy being on the Strand, as opposed to Simpson's on Piccadilly, which is a department store that houses Fortnam and Mason's. Good for American-style ice-cream sodas when you get homesick, which will probably be almost immediately. The Savoy Theatre is in the hotel. Gilbert and Sullivan premiered their operettas there; hence the term 'Savoyards' for those who perform in them. I feel like a human Baedeker. I must be boring you to tears."

"No, you're not. Really you're not. I've never been abroad in my life. I know something about England, mostly London, really, because we've a large British colony in Hollywood."

"Yes, I know. I met most of them at a reception Marion Davies held for me at her Malibu Beach house."

"I *am* impressed. The house is in Santa Monica."

"Is there a difference? It's all sand and infidelities."

Bette laughed. "You learned a lot in just two short weeks."

"It was two long weeks. I was very bored between séances."

"Séances? There were séances?"

"Forgive me, my dear. You didn't recognize my name."

Bette was rarely flustered, but this was one of those times. "If you tell me you're an international celebrity, I shall jump overboard. I have to admit that when not reading scripts or the trade dailies, I don't do much other reading."

"Quite understandable, my dear. You're an actress, and that covers a multitude of sins." She hastened to add, "And I'm not talking down to you or insulting you. I have an aunt who's an actress, quite old and feeble now, if she hasn't passed away in my absence. Well, she's a dear old thing and was quite beautiful and quite popular at one time, but she once admitted that she read nothing but plays and theatrical magazines and on occasion would try reading a recipe, but gave that up as a lost cause because she couldn't decipher them. Anyway, as I told you, I am Nydia Tilson. I'm a world-renowned medium. I don't indulge in séances as often as I used to, for the delicious reason that my incredibly wealthy husband, Ogden, had the good sense to pass away five years ago and leave me with an obscenely incredible fortune and a charming lover. I assume he'll still be charming when I arrive back in London."

Bette was astonished at the woman's candor on such short acquaintance and said so.

Nydia smiled. "There's an aura above you. Not about you, but above you. On deck, even in the fog, I saw it distinctly. This aura marks you as being someone very special."

"I don't feel very special."

"Of course you do. Why else are you fighting for your professional survival? I've read about it in the papers, and when I did I wanted to find you and say, 'Bravo!' It's about time more of our sex fought for our rights. I applaud you, Bette Davis, and it delights me to tell you as much."

The tea arrived, and after it was served and they began helping themselves, Bette said on the spur of the moment, "I wonder . . ."

"Yes?"

"On such short acquaintance, do I dare ask you to help me to find a furnished house? Quite honestly, I can't afford the Savoy for too long, and if I'm to be here for the length of time I suspect I'll have to stay, I'd like the comfort of my own kitchen. I love to cook, you see, and I don't much like dining out on my own. I don't know many people here, and . . ."

"My dear," Nydia interrupted swiftly and without apologizing, "you just might be in luck. I do know a house that will soon be available. It's a charming old thing in St. John's

Wood, in Blenheim Terrace. The Terrace is a cul-de-sac, you know, what you Americans call a dead-end street. It's owned by a very good friend of mine and next door to a house owned by another good friend, a dear, really, a writer. Of course, eccentric and very partial to eating apples but really a dear puss. The house I have in mind for you is owned by a world-famous archeologist."

"Oh, God. I probably haven't heard of him either."

"Probably not. I suppose you haven't heard of Virgil Wynn?"

"If I admit I haven't, will we stay friends?"

Nydia laughed. "Don't you ever riffle the pages of the *National Geographic*?"

"Oh, yes! In my dentist's office!" She continued after a sip of tea, "What is it that possesses a person to poke around in old graves? I'm sure they're dank and fetid and depressing."

"They also contain priceless treasures."

"And archeologists claim them?" She didn't wait for an answer. Nydia would grow accustomed to this annoying shortcoming. "Don't they belong to the country in which they were excavated?"

"In theory they do."

"Not by law?"

"Well, archeologists and local officials play sort of a game of pat-a-cake with each other. Some of the loot is deposited with a local museum. That's to assuage any guilt. Some good pieces are given to the officials themselves to resell to collectors for a very good price, usually."

"That's bribery."

Nydia shrugged. "In order to acquire wealth, one must learn not to be naive."

"That's good. I must remember that."

Nydia continued the lesson in exotic thievery. "A good portion of the find is given to museums. The British Museum bulges at the walls with stolen goods. And finally, a very wise archeologist who knows the value of a pound keeps some of the best pieces for himself."

"I gather that's how Virgil Wynn acquired his fortune."

"As ye gather, so shall ye reap. Virgil's also a shrewd investor. He's shared some incredible tips with me."

Bette said eagerly, "I hope our friendship blossoms to the point where you'll share some with me!"

"How wistful you sound."

"I just can't hold on to a buck. Sixteen hundred dollars a week sounds like a windfall to the initiated. But by the time my agent and my manager take their share, and my accountant and the household help, and with the money it costs to look like what a movie star is supposed to look like in public—" she paused to exhale—"what a sorrowful situation." She flagged a waiter to ask him to get her a pack of cigarettes.

"Don't you like mine?" asked Nydia.

"Oh, of course I do, but like all addicted smokers, I prefer my own brand. Are you sure Mr. Wynn will want to sublet his home to me?" She didn't wait for an answer. "I mean all those treasures he must have on the premises."

"Lots of treasures, all over the house, and wait till you see what he has in his basement. Rest assured, my dear, he is heavily insured against theft."

Nydia got her first taste of Bette's New England practicality. "Oh, my God. Who does the dusting?"

Nydia smiled. "Another treasure. Nellie Mamby. She's Virgil's housekeeper. She also bosses him around, although he's totally unaware of it."

Bette had earlier come to a conclusion about Nydia and Virgil Webb. "Are you very much in love with him?"

Nydia sighed. "I was right when I said you are someone special. You're very clever at deductions, aren't you."

"I'm a Down Easter."

"Is that some special organization? Can anyone join?"

"At last! Something *you* haven't heard of. We refer to New

England as 'Down East.' That's me, a Down Easter, and proud of it."

"In answer to your question, if you still want it . . ."

"I do," responded Bette forthrightly.

"I am not very much in love with him. Virgil isn't the kind of man who arouses any grand passions. He's about forty and attractive and very rich, but then, so am I very rich."

"And very attractive, and I refuse to guess your age."

"Don't be coy. I'm thirty . . . er . . . seven . . . or so. To hell with it." She waved her age away and poured more tea. "What Virgil is, he's solid as a rock. He's dependable. And very generous. He supports his family." She told Bette about Sir Roland and sister Anthea and brother Oscar.

Bette said, "We have that in common." She ticked off on her fingers. "There's my mother; my sister, Barbara; my mother's sister, Mildred; and between jobs, which happens frequently, I support my husband. He's a struggling band-leader."

"Why isn't he back home struggling?"

"He soon will be. We're getting divorced."

"How marvelous, my dear! I'll get the word out you're a free soul and you'll be inundated. Englishmen are terribly partial to actresses! I'm referring to rich Englishmen, and there's still a good proportion of them around and available. And those that aren't available can usually be converted. Yes, I can see by the aura above you you're going to do splendidly in London."

"Have mercy, Nydia. I don't feel like a new man just yet."

Nydia waved the statement away to the same limbo to which she had consigned her age. "You will. Just give your emotional reservoir a little time to refill. Virgil knows a lot of availabilities. Too bad he's going away."

"No it isn't! I want his house!"

Nydia's face reflected concern. "I hope he's feeling better."

"He's been ill?"

Nydia lit a cigarette while the waiter presented Bette with a package of the brand she had requested. Bette tore open the package. Nydia repositioned herself and crossed her legs. "The doctors can't diagnose it. His own and some specialists called in for consultation."

"What are the symptoms?" Bette was genuinely interested, albeit selfishly. She didn't want illness to deter Virgil's departure. She wanted his house with the tenaciousness she would devote to attempting to secure her freedom from Jack Warner's bondage.

"He's been having abdominal pains, accompanied by loss of appetite and fainting spells. And the poor darling is so vain; his hair has begun to thin, and though they're not celebrated for it, the Wynns do have marvelous heads of hair." She made it sound like a cosmetic triumph. "Of course, that was weeks ago before I left. Perhaps it's all cleared up by now. I haven't heard anything since I departed. Virgil's a very poor correspondent. I'm sure if he was dead it would have been in the newspapers. I mean, you do gather that in his own field Virgil is quite the celebrity."

Said Bette wryly, "Yes, that's been permanently established."

"I've been beginning to wonder if what they say about curses can come true."

Bette was intrigued. "What about curses?"

Nydia told her about the legend of a curse supposed to plague those who gut the tombs of Egypt's ancestors.

Bette was mesmerized. "I wish Jack Warner would go to Egypt and open a tomb."

"Hardly likely." Nydia paused and stared into space. After a few moments, she spoke in earnest. "Virgil's father, Lord Roland, thinks he was cursed for having uncovered the tomb of Queen Baramar. She was seemingly quite an obscure queen, dating a long way back in the b.c.'s. Actually, Lord Roland came upon her tomb quite by accident. There was an earthquake in the Valley of the Kings." Bette looked puzzled, so Nydia took a few moments to fill her in on the Valley of

15

the Kings. "Anyway, there was this earthquake, and when the dust had cleared, *voilá!* There was the entrance to her tomb. Lord Roland, of course, was overjoyed, despite a few fatalities among the members of his crew. Of course, he had no idea whose tomb this was until they got to the interior and deciphered the hieroglyphics on the wall, a great many of which were quite obscene."

"Oh, what fun!"

"How'd you guess? Baramar, it seems, was a brazen hussy who took to sex the way your Eleanor Powell takes to tap dancing. My dear! The positions she invented! Lord Roland tried to promote a book of them, but no publisher would dare print it. The Church of England can be so tiresome about that sort of thing. Roland made a great deal of lolly . . ." Bette was puzzled again. ". . . money, dear, money . . . by selling replicas of the walls to a lot of seamy establishments throughout Europe and Asia, but he was profligate in his life-style and was soon drowning in debt. By this time Virgil was establishing himself and threw Pater a life preserver. But Roland never retrieved his luck. So now he's a terribly bitter old man.

"Baramar made headlines when Roland discovered her, and Baramar won him his knighthood. Fourteen years ago, in 1922, the discovery of King Tutankhamon's tomb by Howard Carter and Lord Carnarvon soon turned Roland into a has-been."

"How sad."

"It is, really, because he's quite a decent sort. Eton and Cambridge." They sounded to Bette like a dance team, but she refrained from any comment. "He couldn't raise a dime for any further expeditions. He's called on to lecture occasionally and to do some speaking on the wireless. That keeps him from going round the bend."

"Dare I ask?" Bette was chain-smoking.

"Ask what?"

"Didn't Virgil offer to finance his father?"

"Virgil needed, and still needs, to finance himself. Your

American explorers usually have access to museums and wealthy universities. But here there's not very much of that. And now, with the great worldwide depression, funds grow scarcer and scarcer."

"What happened to the men who unearthed the unpronounceable?"

"Tutankhamon?"

"How I admire the way it trips off your tongue."

"Dear Bette, he's more frequently referred to as King Tut, as in 'Tut tut.' " She waved some cigarette smoke away. "There was indeed a curse on Tut's tomb. Lord Carnarvon was dead within a year. He was a great believer in the occult, very big on séances and mystic symbols. I've been trying to contact him for years, but he remains elusive. Probably too embarrassed by the way he died to come forward like a man and reveal himself." She leaned forward and said darkly, "He died of a mosquito bite."

"You're pulling my leg."

"Not at all. Listen to this." She had Bette's undivided attention. "A soothsayer in Cairo warned Carnarvon to stay out of the Valley of the Kings. So Carnarvon decided to head back to London. Well, as luck would have it, his partner, Howard Carter, used some very heavy persuasion to get him to change his mind. Carnarvon had the money, Carter didn't have a sou."

"So he strong-armed him to continue the expedition."

"Exactly."

"So what happened?"

Nydia was pleased to see Bette so intrigued by her narrative. "After the tomb was opened, and world acclaim and notoriety showered down on them, Lord Carnarvon was bitten by the mosquito."

"Malarial?"

"No, just an ordinary, unprepossessing nuisance. The mosquito bit him on the cheek. The area flared up and a pus pimple formed. While shaving, Carnarvon's razor cut across the pimple, and it became infected. With the infection came a fever, and it turned dangerous. His doctor treated the infection, or at least thought he was treating it, but Carnarvon continued to be seriously ill. And here's the weirdest part. Several hours before he died, he went to see a movie!"

"Oh, good for him!" Bette was pleased to hear Carnarvon had been a movie fan.

"Rudolph Valentino in *The Sheik.*"

"How ironic!"

"Yes. The film was set in Egypt, and it was Egypt that did Carnarvon in."

"What about Howard Carter? How did the curse affect him?"

"Oblivion. The same ugly fate as Lord Roland's. Howard's a wizened, sad old man living in a flat in the Albert Mansions, across from Albert Hall. I'm told he mumbles to himself a great deal these days."

"Probably because he has no one else to talk to."

"Lord Roland visits him occasionally, Virgil's told me. I sometimes think there should be a home for aging archeologists." Her face brightened. "But I must say, and I've told this to Virgil, who finds it perverse, I find the idea of a curse very romantic."

"I find it spooky. The very thought of a curse frightens me."

"My dear, just look upon them as legends. And legends can be *so* romantic."

"I intend to be a legend." Bette's arms were folded, and her look of determination impressed Nydia Tilson.

"The aura over your head tells me you will be."

"I'm serious about that."

"So am I."

"I know I've got what it takes to make it to the very top of my profession. I'm determined to win a genuine Oscar."

"Who's Oscar?"

"It's my name for the Academy Award. When I received

mine, I said it looked like my Uncle Oscar and I was quoted around the world."

"Somehow I think it missed the United Kingdom."

"No it didn't. The whole world knows what an Oscar is."

"If you say so, I most certainly believe you." Friend or no friend, Nydia recognized Bette Davis as a woman of formidable ambition and possessed of the necessary ruthlessness to realize that ambition. "Now, what's a genuine Oscar as opposed to your everyday, run-of-the-mill Oscar?"

"Did you see my performance as Mildred two years ago in *Of Human Bondage?*"

"Absolutely brilliant!" And she meant it.

Bette said heatedly, "I should have gotten an Oscar *then*. But no! I was done out of it! Jack Warner forced people to vote against me to keep me in line, to keep me in bad roles in bad pictures so he wouldn't have to pay me more money! And I'm indentured to him until 1942! Can you beat that? 1942!"

"Fate can be so cruel."

"So Jack made me do *Dangerous*. I played an alcoholic actress based on the late Jeanne Eagels."

"I seem to have heard of her."

"She was quite good. She made a few films. She drank herself and drugged herself to death in 1929."

"That was a bad year for a lot of people."

"Christ, how I overacted that part. And for that piece of garbage they voted me an Oscar! The consolation prize!"

"Don't be so hard on yourself, Bette. I'm sure you were quite good or you wouldn't have been honored. Hollywood can't be that foolish or hypercritical."

"Ha ha ha."

The mockery brought a smile to Nydia's lips. It brought back the memory of her two weeks in Hollywood. She confided to Bette, "The séance I held for Marion Davies was also a mockery. She wanted me to reach the silent-screen director Thomas Ince, who, it was rumored, was shot to death by Hearst many years ago during a yachting trip. She wanted Ince to tell the truth, that it was a diseased ulcer that killed him."

"Were you able to contact Ince?"

"No. It seems he was busy elsewhere. But one of her guests confided in me that your gossip columnist Louella Parsons was a witness to the killing and in return for her silence was made one of the most powerful women in the cinema."

"Poor old Lolly. Her husband's an alcoholic, her daughter's a lesbian, or so I've been told, and she herself is incontinent. Ruth Chatterton won't have her at her house because she leaves stains on the sofa and it always has to be recovered. Ruth was a star at Warners. They dropped her last year. They said she was too old. She's over forty."

"How nasty. Perhaps the Warners haven't read Walter Pitkin's *Life Begins at Forty.*"

"Hollywood producers don't read anything except the fine print in contracts." She rubbed out a cigarette in a tray. "I guess I should get back to the cabin and try to behave like a wife, albeit an estranged one. . . . Nydia?"

"Yes, dear?"

"I know it's awfully short notice, but you really are a friend, aren't you?"

"Short of taking a blood oath, you shall be convinced, Bette."

"You see, now that I've made two serious breaks in my life, with the studio and with my husband, I'm beginning to realize the enormity of these decisions. I'm a little frightened."

"There's no need to be. Your aura will protect you."

"I wish I could be as sure of my aura as you are."

"Trust me."

And instinct told Bette Davis to trust Nydia Tilson.

2

BETTE SILENTLY ADMIRED HAM NELSON for trying to put a brave face on their situation. They were huddled together on a platform in Waterloo Station from which the train to South-ampton was scheduled to depart. There wasn't much time left and Bette was babbling small talk that got smaller and smaller as time ticked by. His luggage was already on board and he wished he was. This parting was too painful and he still suffered from a slight fever.

"God, what awful memories this place brings back to me." Her hand, holding a cigarette, was making circles and they were dizzying.

"You've never been here before." He nervously rolled and unrolled a copy of the *Tatler*.

"Oh, yes I have. One of the first movies I made at Universal. *Waterloo Bridge.*" She puffed the cigarette. "Mae Clarke did the lead. It should have been me. It did nothing for Mae. It took Jimmy Cagney pushing half a grapefruit into her face in *Public Enemy* to give her any recognition." She dropped the cigarette and crushed it with her shoe. "I'm babbling away like a madwoman. Why don't you tell me to shut up?"

He ignored the welcome suggestion like the gentleman he was. "I'm glad you've met Nydia Tilson. At least you have one friend here you can be sure of."

"Yes. She's marvelous." She looked at her wristwatch. "I'm meeting her in half an hour. She's taking me to meet Virgil Wynn. I hope he approves of me. I must say, thanks to Nydia I'm getting quite an impressive education in archeology. You know, sort of learning the artifacts of life." She laughed nervously. "Bad joke. Anyway, it should be the artifacts of death. The Egyptians believe in reincarnation. Do you think we lived in another life?"

"I hope not. It's tough enough living in this one." The train whistle blew. The conductor blew his whistle. Passengers hurried to board the train and get into their compartments. Ham's was second-class, Bette being practical again. The engine was gathering a head of steam, and past Ham, Bette could see the engineer hanging over the side of his cab, impatient for the boarding to be completed. Ham put his arms around Bette and hugged her tightly. "Don't let them frighten you."

"I won't."

"You're a scrapper, honey. You're Ruthie's daughter. Live up to the family tradition."

"I will."

Ham stepped back. She hoped he wasn't going to go all teary on her. He was terribly sentimental. "See you soon."

"I'm not sure when. The court hearing isn't until October fourteenth."

"Trust Sir William." Sir William Jowitt was Bette's very expensive lawyer.

"At his fees, I have to. If all goes well with Virgil Wynn, I'll cable you the address and phone number."

He kissed her cheek and then hurried to board the train.

"Ham!" she shouted. He stood in the doorway hoping she was about to ask him not to leave. "Call my mother the minute you get back and take her to dinner!" The train was moving, and Bette tried to keep up with it as it slowly gained speed. "Tell her all about the curses! She'll love it! And about Nydia, except she might get jealous. She's so possessive!" The train was beginning to outdistance her. She stood still, waving her hand. The train and her husband were growing smaller and smaller. Bette lit a cigarette. Even she found it difficult to watch her past disappearing into the future. Slowly and contemplatively she left the platform. She was meeting Nydia Tilson at Virgil Wynn's mansion. Her pace quickened as she crossed the main hall of the cavernous Waterloo Station searching for the taxi rank. Her troubled thoughts were clashing against each other. Jack Warner. Sir William Jowitt. Ham Nelson. Nydia Tilson. Virgil Wynn. Alone in London. There was a line of arriving passengers waiting for the taxis to pull in. Bette decided to try her luck farther down the street, and it was a wise move. She gave the driver the address and then settled back as the taxi headed for Waterloo Bridge and the general direction of St. John's Wood.

Twenty minutes later, she stood in front of a brick wall that spanned the width of Blenheim Terrace. In front, to her left, was a solid wooden door that led to the Wynn mansion, and to her right was a wrought-iron gate that led to his neighbor's less imposing home. Bette tried the left latch. The door creaked open inward. A long path of bricks very artfully cemented together led to the front door. Bette stood still for a moment and partook of the atmosphere and her surroundings. Awfully large mansion, she thought, maybe too big for her to be knocking around in. If she knew enough people, she could hold a ball, but fat chance of that happening. On either side of the front door there were tall French windows, heavily draped. The drapes were closed but Bette saw one open a smidgen. She was being examined and it made her nervous. She resisted the urge to light up, considering that making an entrance with a cigarette dangling from her mouth was more in Jean Harlow's line. The grounds were beautifully landscaped. Nydia had told her that in the back there were lovely gardens populated with flora and Egyptian artifacts in equal proportions. She wondered if Virgil ever considered a dig in his own gardens. He might turn up something interesting, other than a dog's bone.

Yes. She had been watched. The door was opening slowly, propelled by an unseen hand, like the opening of a movie thriller, and she half-expected to hear a blood-curdling scream. Instead she saw a tall, good-looking woman with patrician, albeit sharp, features. Her bearing was majestic, as though she might be royalty. Her mouth was parted in a toothy grin. If this is the housekeeper, thought Bette, I'll be damned if she expects to outclass me. Bette smiled and asked, "Is this Nellie Mamby?"

"No, my dear." She advanced a few steps with hand outstretched. Bette shook her hand. "Mamby's in the kitchen preparing tea. I'm Anthea Wynn, Virgil's sister. He sent me to greet you. Nydia's arrived and they are chatting in the living room. I live nearby, so I'm always underfoot." Bette's heart sank. "But once Virgil leaves, I shall resume writing my blank verse, which too often results in blank spaces." She favored Bette with something Bette assumed was meant to be a chuckle. Bette followed Anthea into the impressive hall. "Virgil's not been well, but now that Nydia's back, he's improving. Nydia, you will undoubtedly learn, is all for improvements." She pointed to a chair that boasted fine carvings. "Why don't you leave your things on this chair? It dates back to only about 15 B.C."

"Oh. A Johnny-come-lately."

She heard Nydia's melodic voice. "You're here, my dear, you're here at last. Come meet Virgil; he's all atip with anticipation." Anthea stood to one side in the doorway of the living room, indicating that Bette should precede her. This, thought Bette, is a weird one. Nydia crossed the magnificent room with hands outstretched.

"Oh, dear, dear, dear. You do look a bit peak-ed. Was Waterloo Station all that traumatic?"

"No, the station was impressive. It was my husband's departure that was traumatic. So this is Virgil Wynn! I've heard so much about you!"

"And I assure you, it's all true." He kissed her hand.

Bette was startled as Nydia favored her with a sly wink. Bette was thinking, This man looks awful. Sunken cheeks, dark circles under his eyes, sickly, sallow skin. She wondered if he could make it to the bathroom, let alone Egypt. She said cheerfully, "I must say, what I've seen so far of your home is most impressive."

"Well, it's just the years of accumulation," he said modestly.

"Accumulation! You call all this accumulation?" She was making a sweeping gesture and missed by a hair knocking over a table lamp. "These are the treasures of Xanadu!" She thought for a moment. "Is Xanadu correct?"

"Of course Xanadu's correct," said Nydia. "Kublai Khan and all that. Ah! Here's Mamby with the tea!"

Mamby was pushing the tea cart in front of her. The small woman reminded Bette of the character actress Una O'Connor, who was a much-sought-after shrieker for horror films. Virgil introduced them and they exchanged the proper amenities. Bette felt assured they would like each other. Mamby settled the cart in front of Nydia, who exclaimed, "Oh, dear! Am I to be Mother? Anthea, wouldn't you prefer to do the honors?"

"As a matter of fact, no. I want to get to know Bette better. My dear, do I make you nervous staring at you?"

"I'm an actress, Miss Wynn. It is Miss Wynn, isn't it?"

"I'd prefer you called me Anthea and that I should call you Bette."

" 'Bett—eeee,' not 'Bet.' Nydia pronounces it 'Bet' too. It's 'Bett . . . eee.' "

"Oh, dear," said Anthea. "I shall never get used to that. 'Bett-eeee' is spelled with a 'y.' When it's not, we say 'Bet,' as in Balzac's Cousine Bette."

"What about Irene Dunne?" countered Bette. "Do you pronounce her name 'Eye-reen-eee Dun-neeee'?" She thought she saw daggers in Anthea's eyes as Nydia poured and Mamby served, offering milk or lemon.

"Oh, Bette, stop being a tease," admonished Nydia, as she cast a sly glance at Virgil. How awful he looks. He's so much thinner since before I went to California. He's cadaverish. He will die in Egypt, if he ever gets there, and he's got to get there because I can see Bette has her heart set on this house.

"Anthea, you asked if I mind being stared at. Well, you do it so subtly, I don't mind at all. Actually, as an actress, constantly in the spotlight, I expect to be stared at. Oh, damn it, that sounded so pretentious! Well, let me tell you the truth. It's when the public stops staring that I'll start worrying. Virgil, you've had such a fantastic career. I knew so little about you until I met Nydia on the boat. She's quite proud of you."

"Are you really, Nydia?"

Nydia took center stage. "Of course I am. You know I am. I'm always bragging that I know you. And now I brag that I know Bette Davis. My cup runneth over. Is everyone served?"

"Yes, ma'am," said Nellie Mamby as she moved among the others with plates of biscuits and finger-sized sandwiches of ham paste and thinly sliced cucumber.

Bette suddenly shivered and almost spilled her tea.

Concerned, Nydia asked, "Bette, what's wrong?"

"I really don't know," she replied as she placed the cup and saucer carefully on the table at her elbow. "I guess somebody's walked over my grave." She was aware of the sudden silence. "I must explain. That's an old American expression."

"Most frequently spoken, I should think," offered Virgil, "by old Americans."

Anthea had moved to a window, and as she sipped her tea she looked out. "Curiosity has gotten the better of her again." She was referring to Virgil's neighbor, who was in her garden pruning some bushes between bites of an apple, which she placed on a small wooden stool when resuming pruning.

Virgil explained to Bette, "She's referring to my neighbor, Mrs. Mallowan. She writes books. Her husband, Max Mallowan, is also an archeologist."

"How coincidental!" exclaimed Bette.

"Not really. Max and my father are good friends, and so he has become a friend of mine. I recommended their house to them and I was quite pleased when they elected to move in. They're charming company. Max is away on a dig in Mesopotamia."

Bette asked with curiosity, "Don't you ever do your exploring closer to home?"

"I am a confirmed Egyptologist. Like my father, who is rather retired, I'm afraid, albeit reluctantly."

"If he's still raring to go," said Bette, "why don't you invite him along on this trip?"

"As a matter of fact, I have, but Sir Roland, my father, is not interested in the Ptolemys. And they have me hypnotized from the far and mysterious recesses of their graves." Mamby excused herself rather than suffer another of Virgil's dissertations on the Ptolemy kings. Bette was genuinely interested in hearing about them. Virgil spoke slowly and carefully. He was in his element. As he droned on, Anthea passed among them freshening their tea, while Nydia dwelled on Virgil's frightening disability. She wanted to throw her arms around him and reassure him his health would soon return, that there are no such things as Egyptian curses, and ask whether he had really extended an invitation to Sir Roland to accompany him on this trip. "My dear Bette," she heard Virgil saying, "I think I have you transfixed."

"This is all so fascinating. This is all so new to me. Oh, how I wish I could go with you!"

"Then who'd there be to occupy my house? Come! It's time you saw the rest of it. I won't trouble you with the basement."

"Oh, I adore basements. Especially when they have bargains." To his perplexed expression, she quickly explained American department stores and bargain basements.

"What a lovely custom," said Anthea. "I wish we had those here. I love to buy things on the cheap."

Nydia tried to get Virgil to let her and Anthea conduct the

tour while he remained behind and conserved his strength, but Virgil was having none of it. He was fascinated by the Hollywood movie star, with her startlingly oversized eyes and her unusual mouth, which turned down at the corners; her short, sharp, quick gestures; the way she tamed a lighted cigarette. There was nothing like her in either England or Egypt, and probably, for that matter, anywhere else on earth.

They slowly traveled from floor to floor and from room to room. There were three floors and at least a total of twenty rooms. Bette chose a bedroom on the first floor and was surprised to hear it had once been Anthea's. Bette complimented her on her exquisite taste and was rewarded with another toothy grin. In the course of the tour, Bette learned that Virgil's father and brother, Oscar, had also lived in the house but did not question why the father and the two siblings now occupied their own residences. Bette could see that Virgil had once been quite an attractive man. His manners were impeccable; his voice was beautifully modulated and when he spoke of Baramar and her pornography, Bette began to feel a familiar stirring that made her wonder if she hadn't been too rash in sending her husband packing. The kitchen, she was warned by Nydia, was Mamby's private enclave and guarded with an unbecoming possessiveness. Betty filed a mental note that Mamby would have to recognize that Bette Davis was a Down Easter and a hell of a good cook, especially with shellfish. Her clam chowder was usually spoken of in hushed tones, or else.

Now it was time to explore the grounds. Again, as in the front of the estate, the landscaping was superlative. Bette clapped her hands with delight. "Oh, I shall be strolling here every day when I'm not busy fighting in the courts. But how do these flowers and shrubberies thrive in this dismal climate?" No one took offense at her comment about the climate.

Virgil explained, "London is near the Gulf Stream, as of course is much of this region, and so the flora flourishes all year round. The United Kingdom is mostly verdant. In fact, you might try to find the time to travel south to Cornwall and take the boat to the Scilly Islands. That's where the flora is truly exquisite. It has the lushness of the tropics. My dear, you're trembling again. Is it too chilly for you?"

"No, not at all. Really . . ." What she wouldn't tell him was that she was experiencing a presentiment. She might have said, rather darkly, something like "Heavy, heavy hangs over my head." Was it the forthcoming court action? She didn't think it was that at all. Was it something about Nydia? No, Nydia was too preoccupied with worrying about Virgil's health. Was it Anthea? There was something brooding and foreboding about Anthea. Something unhealthy about her devotion to her brother. The insinuation that it was Anthea who presided at teatime and probably at dinner parties and receptions. And Anthea was still staring at her. Not so obviously now, but staring nevertheless. She hoped she wasn't a mind reader. Why were Anthea and the others no longer in residence? Why was Bette suddenly so interested? Because of her feeling of unease out here in the open. Anthea had wished for a bargain basement. It suddenly occurred to Bette that Anthea and the others were dependent on Virgil for their economic survival. She hoped that under that smooth and suave facade Virgil wasn't mean and brutish. She'd seen too much of that in Hollywood, where just about everyone was being suffocated by the financial dependence of relatives. Including Bette Davis.

An immense privet hedge separated the grounds of the two estates, and on her side of the hedge Mrs. Mallowan was straining to hear what was being said on the other side. She recognized the voices of Virgil and Anthea and, of course, Nydia, who was a good personal friend, but the fourth voice remained enigmatic. She caught snatches of clues that indicated the young woman was an actress of sorts, in fact, a movie actress of sorts, and what's more, a Hollywood movie actress of sorts. The voice was too mature to be that darling little Shirley Temple. It was too American to be either Garbo or Dietrich, two stars to whom Mrs. Mallowan was deeply devoted. It wasn't a sophisticated voice like that of Constance Bennett, who, she had read, was filming in London. There was a gate at the end of the privet hedge, and she wondered about making her way to it and somewhat subtly inviting herself to join the group. Of course, she wouldn't deign to explain that while listening to them she had had one of her frequent presentiments, which were usually pretty precise and accurate. She heard the actress being delighted at the prospect of moving into the Wynn house the coming Saturday. So the actress was to be her new neighbor. She sounded all right, and Agatha Mallowan liked actresses. She was crazy about the monologist Ruth Draper, who had inspired *Lord Edgeware Dies*. Of course, in private she didn't consider Ruth Draper a *real* actress. She was a monologist, and monologists are on stage talking to themselves while permitting the audience to eavesdrop. She heard Nydia say she would help 'Bet' move from the Savoy on Saturday morning.

The Savoy?

Well, she had to have some form of wealth. The Savoy wasn't exactly a boardinghouse in Blackpool. She was at the gate, and in her most ingratiating way she called out to the group, "I say, Nydia, is that you?"

"Of course, darling. How are you? I was going to drop by for a minute with my new American friend, Bette Davis."

"Oh, of course," said Mrs. Mallowan with unrestrained pleasure. "Now I recognize her. My dear, you were so impressive in *Of Human Bondage*. And how cleverly you mastered the cockney accent!"

Nydia introduced them, and Bette liked the middle-aged woman at once. "I worked like a slave to get it right," said Bette. "And how kind of you to applaud the effort."

"I always try to be kind, my dear. So, Virgil, you're really off to Egypt!"

"Saturday morning, my dear. Back to the Valley of the Kings."

"Lucky man. I ache so to do another dig with my Max. I'm planning a story set in Egypt." She said to Bette: "Egypt is so fascinating. So mysterious and so filthy. Billions of flies, my dear, billions. And the poverty is horrifying. But the atmosphere! Inconceivable! The Sphinx. The Pyramids. And the Nile with its little boats and its crocodiles. Don't let me go on. Virgil, be sure to see me before you go. And I assure you, dear man, I shall be a very good neighbor to Miss Davis, if she will let me."

Bette took the woman's hand and gently squeezed it. "Mrs. Mallowan, I can use all the good neighbors that can be spared."

Mrs. Mallowan said, "You and Nydia must drop by later. There'll be tea, unless you're waterlogged. Otherwise some sherry. Or perhaps we'll be devil-may-care with whisky." She was moving away from the gate, smiling and satisfied. She felt she had carried that off very smoothly and decided to reward herself with a slice of Dundee cake.

As Bette and the others walked back into the house, Bette said, "Isn't she a charmer! This must be my lucky day. This house and a lovely neighbor; what a wonderful package."

Nydia said, "Now to the tiresome details of the rent."

Bette said with an edge to her voice, "Shouldn't that be between Virgil and myself?"

"There's little need for tiresome details," interjected Virgil. He said to Bette, "Nellie Mamby is paid ten pounds a week."

"Much too much," commented Anthea with an imperious sniff.

Bette was doing some fast arithmetic and converted ten pounds to fifty dollars. Fifty dollars for a cook, housekeeper, and all-around factotum. She restrained herself from shouting, "But what a steal!" Instead she said, "I'm agreeable to that."

Virgil smiled. "Then there's the telephone, the gas and electricity, and the rubbish collector. Now, as to the rent . . ." Behind her back, Bette hid crossed fingers. ". . . I consider it my jolly good luck to have you looking after my house and my treasures for me."

"Bette," said Nydia warmly, "your jaw has dropped." Anthea's had also dropped, but for a different reason.

"I can't let you do that!" Bette was truly astonished.

"My dear," said Virgil, not realizing he sounded like Ronald Colman, "don't be tiresome. It bothered me to think of Nellie alone in this old mausoleum." Except for Anthea underfoot, and probably taking an inventory, thought Bette.

"It is not a mausoleum," chirruped Nydia. "It's a lovely old thing, and I wish it were mine."

"It could have been," said Virgil softly.

"Now, now, darling," Nydia cautioned. "It isn't healthy to dwell on what might have been. Isn't that so, Bette?"

"You're reading my mind. I've got some 'might have been' of my own to dwell on." She hoped Ham would find his second-class cabin suitable.

Anthea's voice was next. "Virgil, you look done in. You should have your medicine and then a nap."

Virgil turned on her smartly. "How often have I told you you should have been the overseer of a plantation in Malaya?" He said to the other two women, "Anthea tends to get very bossy, very imperious. I find that most unbecoming in a woman."

Bette was thinking, He should thank God he's not living with me.

Nellie Mamby came bustling in. "It's time for your medicine and your nap."

Bette caught Virgil's eye and giggled. She said, "This will all soon be behind you."

"Quite right," he agreed. "Now, Bette, to get out of your way and give Nellie the time to tidy up for your Saturday move, I shall spend Friday night at my club. Actually, I'm having dinner with my father and some friends, and it is convenient for me to stay there. My belongings are to be picked up Friday afternoon. I'm so looking forward to the voyage through the Med. Ah, the thought of peace!" Anthea flashed him a look that did not escape Bette's notice. Virgil sounded annoyed as he addressed Nellie Mamby. "I'll be upstairs in a few moments, Nellie. There's no need to wait for me."

"I'll see you Saturday morning, Mamby." Bette hoped Mamby would be glad to see her.

"I'm looking forward to that, Miss Bette," wisely pronounced 'Bet-tee.' Bette left the room with a deliberately measured pace.

Anthea spoke up. "If you like, Bette, I could be here Saturday morning and lend a hand."

Bette said swiftly, "There's no need to trouble yourself. Nydia's picking me up at the Savoy, and after we drop my stuff off we're lunching with George Arliss."

This was all news to Nydia, who didn't mind one bit. She was proud of Bette for letting everyone answer her questions without Bette cutting in and answering them herself. She was proud of Virgil and his generosity towards Bette. She had told him Bette was a bit strapped for cash and carefully husbanding her pennies, but she'd never dreamt he'd turn over the mansion practically rent free. Bette and Nydia exchanged warm goodbyes with Virgil and his sister, wishing Virgil all the luck and good health possible. Virgil led them to the front door, while Anthea stayed behind in the sitting room for a few moments of quiet, if troubled, contemplation.

Virgil watched the two women as they briskly walked down the brick path to the sturdy wooden door, on their way to Mrs. Mallowan's. He stood in his doorway, arms folded, eyes misting. He knew he would never see them again.

From her reception-room window, Mrs. Mallowan could see Bette and Nydia coming through her wrought-iron gate. She remembered the scrupulous care with which Max had selected it at the ironmongers on nearby Abbey Road. Dear Max. She hoped he was taking the prescribed salts for his chronic constipation. Again, as she did several times a day, she thanked her lucky stars for having met and been successfully wooed by Max Mallowan. A vast improvement on her first husband, Archibald Christie. Therefore, could some psychiatrist explain why she continued to sign her books 'by Agatha Christie'?

Agatha flung the door wide. "Ah, my dears! It is so good to welcome you! So, Bette, you move into the house Saturday morning."

"While heaving a huge sigh of relief," said Bette as she removed her coat and sank into a chair.

Agatha did everything but cluck like a mother hen as she asked, "What shall it be? Tea? Several spots of sherry? Scotch whisky?"

Nydia was sitting on the overstuffed sofa. "Let it wait a few moments, Agatha, and sit down." Agatha sat next to Nydia. "Something troubled you in the garden. What was it?"

"Nothing escapes you, does it, Nydia?" She said to Bette. "You know of course, that my dear friend is one of the world's really great mediums. She is very sensitive to people's moods and very sympathetic."

"Thank God for that," agreed Bette. "She was my sounding board for a good part of the voyage here."

Nydia said to Bette, "Something other than sister Anthea was bothering you too." She explained to Agatha, "Twice Bette got sudden shivers. She explained one as someone walking over her grave."

"No one is walking over Bette's grave," said Agatha. To Bette: "You shall live a long, long life."

"Not alone, I hope. I never want to be alone." Bette hoped God heard her and was taking notes.

"I can't help you there, as I shan't be around to comfort you. I'm sure I'm at least two decades older than you."

"What about me, Agatha? About how much longevity do you think I could expect?" asked Nydia.

"You? The rock of Gibraltar? I suspect they'll have to hammer you into your grave."

"Then I shall see to it I leave instructions to be cremated. Well, Bette, what was giving you the shakes?"

"I don't really know if I can explain it. Of course, it might have been the house. It *is* cold and damp."

"All British homes are cold and damp. Virgil's doesn't have to be. He's a bit stingy about using the fireplaces."

"It's all that time he spends digging in a hot climate," said Nydia. "He welcomes the lack of heating in his house." She said to Bette, "You must buy yourself some lovely, warm sweaters. As a matter of fact there's a sale on at Selfridge's." She added wickedly, "We could stop in after lunch with Mr. Arliss."

"Mr. Arliss? You mean George Arliss? You know him?"

"He's a dear friend," Bette told Agatha, "and I haven't looked him up yet. Not him and not a chum from my acting days in New York, Janie Clarkson. I'm really in no hurry to see her. She so resents my success."

"Bette." Nydia nailed the name to her ear. "What was giving you the shakes?"

"It was sort of a presentiment."

"Aha!" Agatha was on her feet and beginning to pace, hands clasped behind her back, look very official and lacking only a meerschaum pipe protruding from her mouth. "I had one too. In the garden before making my presence known to your group. What was your presentiment about, Bette?"

"I swear to you, I really don't know." She paused. "Well, actually, I'm just not sure."

"Out with it," prompted Nydia.

"I guess it was Virgil. I had the feeling I would never see him again. And I want to see him again. He's such a nice man. Nydia, how could you let him escape?"

"I did it rather nonchalantly, much to sister Anthea's relief. Well, Agatha, and what about your presentiment?"

"I know I shall see Virgil again, because he doesn't depart from the house until Friday and that's two days away. But after Friday, I too doubt if I shall see him again. Don't look so tragic, Nydia. You're a clever woman. You're not blind. Virgil does not stand alone. Death is his companion." She searched their faces. "Don't you understand? He is being murdered."

3

"MURDERED?" BETTE WAS DUMBFOUNDED.

"He's probably being poisoned. Very slowly. Over a period of months. Tell me, Nydia, do you know if Virgil is addicted to arsenic?"

"I don't know."

"Strychnine?"

"Again I don't know."

Bette sounded incredulous. "Can people be addicted to poisons? Aren't they always fatal?"

"My dear Bette," said Agatha warmly, "let me add to your education. In small doses, arsenic and strychnine have very soothing, euphoric effects. Why, my dears, sweet old Queen Victoria was addicted to arsenic. And she lived almost forever. Very carefully administered by her physicians, probably, after taking their own doses. Doctors, my dears, tend to be addicted to something or another, it's so easy for them to get their hands on the stuff. That's why, Nydia, I was wondering if Virgil is addicted."

"Damn Virgil. He very well could be. He's always so secretive."

Bette said to Agatha, "Do you mind if I smoke?"

Nydia answered for Agatha. "No, she doesn't, and I want one too. I don't see any ashtrays."

"You'll see them soon enough," said Agatha sweetly. She crossed to a cupboard while the ladies lit up.

"Wouldn't Virgil's doctor know?" asked Bette.

"He could, but he might not want to disclose the information. You see, if Virgil is addicted, it's their secret. What's his doctor's name, Nydia?"

"Solomon Hubbard. He looks after me too, when he can find me. He's blind as a bat and totally inept."

Bette asked with amazement, "Then why do you go to him?"

"So I'll never hear any bad news. He's not really as bad as all that. He keeps me supplied with sleeping draughts the way he probably keeps Virgil supplied with arsenic or strychnine. Don't look at me like that, Agatha. You know they can't be bought over the counter."

"I do know that. But you can buy weed killers and they are very, very poisonous. We've had a lot of people in the U.K. done in with weed killers. We're very big on poisoning, Bette. The Borgias may have been masters at it, but we British have refined poisoning to a fine art." She added thoughtfully, "Both physically and vocally." Nydia was at the phone and dialing. "My dear Nydia, this is terribly rude of you."

"I'm phoning Solomon Hubbard!"

"Are you feeling ill?"

"No, Agatha, I'm not feeling ill. I want to ask him if he's prescribing poisons for Virgil."

"And you expect him to tell you?"

"He's an honest man. Of course he'll tell me."

Agatha was at Nydia's side. She pulled the phone from her hand and plunked it back on the receiver. "My dear Nydia, I'm sure you know doctors cannot reveal what occurs between them and their patients."

"Of course," agreed Bette. "It's part of their hypocritical oath."

"Hippocratical," corrected Agatha. "I sometimes get the words mixed up too."

Bette laughed and then just as quickly stopped laughing as she reminded herself of the gravity of Virgil's tragic situation. "Oh, my God. Agatha! Nydia! Do you suppose Virgil *wants* to die?"

Agatha spoke quietly, carefully measuring her words. "I very much doubt a man leaving on an extended archeological expedition is at the same time working on hastening his mortality. I'm sure in the back of his mind he knows he's dying, and perhaps, like all Egypt, which he so adores, he believes there's a new life awaiting him."

"If so," said Bette with her native practicality, "perhaps he should be buried with a shovel."

The three shared a much-needed laugh. Agatha took matters into her own hands and poured Scotch whisky into three tumblers.

Nydia asked, "Do you suppose Virgil is suffering from a fatal disease, something easily contracted in Egypt? He's told me the place is filthy with diseases, most of them unpronounceable."

"If he is, I'm sure he certainly would have shared that information with you," Agatha reasoned.

"Perhaps. You know, Virgil is a terribly considerate man. He might not want those of us near and dear to him to agonize."

"Also, he's British," Bette reminded them.

"What's that got to do with it?" asked Nydia.

"Stiff upper lip and all that," said Bette matter-of-factly.

Agatha bristled. "There is so much misinformation about us spread around the world! And frankly, my dears, I think it's all Hollywood's fault! The brave, the undefeatable, the unemotional British. The sun never sets and all that rot. I've seen my Max cry; and the good Lord knows I cry; and Nydia, you were an emotional wreck at your husband's funeral, or else you deserve an Academy Award."

"Oh, I was very sincere then," said Nydia as she sipped her whisky. Bette wondered if she dare ask for some ice, and then immediately thought better of it. Mrs. Mallowan did not strike her as the ice type. In fact, she was troubed by the paucity of refrigerators in the country. She had read this in an article about the United Kingdom cut out of *Liberty* magazine by her thoughtful mother in hopes of persuading her to do her lawsuit from someplace a bit more civilized. Bette reminded her mother the English had been civilized long before America. The English had cold larders in which they stored their food, and Bette now wished they'd import master chefs to teach them how to cook the food. And she also wished there was a law against mushy brussels sprouts.

"Stiff upper lip indeed," repeated Agatha. Then: "Well, if he's not addicted, someone is poisoning Virgil."

"Dear God, not really!" cried Nydia. "But who?"

"Hercule Poirot, with his magnificent little gray cells, would have his suspicions. Also, dear Miss Jane Marple would be over there right now snooping about for traces of the poisons in question."

Bette's eyes were popping. "Well, whoever they are, why don't you get in touch with them?"

"Now really, Bette!" Nydia looked impish.

"Now really what?" The recent cigarette had been replaced by a fresh one.

"Hercule Poirot and Jane Marple are two of my creations. Um, you have heard that I write?"

"Why, of course I have. Either Nydia or Virgil mentioned it."

"If it was me, then I didn't mention it hard enough. Poirot and Marple are whizzes at detection."

"Well, Agatha, if they're your counterparts, why don't you start whizzing on Virgil's behalf?"

"Oh, I've been doing that for many months now. Long before Nydia left for the United States."

"Then you must have loads of theories." She sipped her Scotch without taking her eyes from Agatha's face. To Bette's astonishment, Agatha selected an apple from a bowl of fruit and took a healthy bite.

Agatha explained, "I always do my best thinking when I eat apples. You should try it." She was then lost in thought for a while, and the others did not disturb her. She looked from one to the other as she set the remains of the apple aside. "Have either of you heard of Charles Wilson Peale and his son Raphaelle?" They hadn't. "Well, Bette, the elder Peale was one of the fathers of American art. He was most famous for his portrait of George Washington." Bette was wondering if her face was reflecting her hopeless feeling of stupidity. How poorly educated she was! Blast Ruthie for that.

Agatha continued, "But one of his sons outshone him. He was recognized as the foremost American still-life painter of his time. And the elder Peale was soon eaten up with envy and jealousy. The elder Peale's hobby was taxidermy. He developed compounds of arsenic and mercury that enabled him to preserve bird and animal skins for stuffing."

"Oh, no, oh, no, I know what you're getting at."

"Hush, Nydia, and let me finish. He also taught Raphaelle how to do it. Soon, Raphaelle was suffering from upset stomachs, having fainting spells, headaches, loss of hair . . ."

"Virgil has lost so much hair." Bette signaled Nydia to be quiet.

"Raphaelle's teeth loosened and he also suffered from delirium tremens. But that could be attributed to his heavy drinking. The question for us to examine is, did William systematically poison his son because his jealousy drove him insane, or was the poison self-inflicted by Raphaelle, who, despite his fame and wealth, was a very unhappy man?"

"Are you suggesting Sir Roland is poisoning Virgil?" Bette's voice was up an octave. "If so, when has he the opportunity?"

Nydia said, "Nellie Mamby dotes on Sir Roland."

"Not having met him," said Bette, "I've no yardstick to measure his doteability."

Agatha said, "I think Virgil is quite aware he is dying. He's anxious to get back to Egypt to die there. I'll bet he's made provision for it with his solicitor. He's aware he's dying and he knows who's killing him."

Bette was stunned. "Then why doesn't he speak up?"

"He's a gentleman," explained Agatha with disarming simplicity. "Gentlemen avoid scandals, or at least that's the addlebrained code our upper classes live by. I'd be damned if I thought someone was trying to do me in and didn't yell my bloody head off."

Bette couldn't resist. "Didn't Snow White take a bite of the poisoned apple given to her by her wicked stepmother?"

Agatha said, "There are no wicked stepmothers in our immediate vicinity. At least none that I know of. And Snow White was a bit of a ninny."

Nydia downed her whisky and put a brave face on the situation. "My mind's made up. I shall confront Virgil."

"Don't you do any such thing!" cried Agatha. "It will serve no useful purpose. There's no way to rescue him now. He's much too far gone. Remember, my dear, I once served as a nurse. I saw others in his condition. They too were irreversibly ill. And there's no saving Virgil. Believe me, there's no saving him. If he recognizes there's no hope for himself, then let him go in peace. With dignity. In Egypt."

"If he gets there," said Bette.

"I hope he doesn't," said Agatha. "They're not very good about autopsies in warm climates."

"This is so unreal! It's as though I never left Hollywood!"

Agatha was refilling their glasses. "It's very real. You are not in Hollywood. Somewhere among the Wynn household there lurks a killer. And sooner or later, that person will make a mistake, give themselves away, and they'll be unmasked and Virgil avenged."

Bette crossed her legs and placed her hands firmly on her waist. "Has it occurred to you ladies that if the killer thinks we're wised up we could be next as targets?"

"I think we're quite safe," said Agatha confidently. "But there could be others who aren't. Still, all we can do is await further developments. Nydia, will you be seeing Virgil before he leaves?"

"No. He's sequestering himself until his dinner appointment Friday night."

"That's good. Why don't you two go to a movie tonight? There's a charming new Jessie Matthews on in Leicester Square. *It's Love Again.* I find her so charming despite her minimal talent. I saw it the other afternoon." She sang in a reedy but brave soprano, "It's love again, it's love again . . ." and just as suddenly broke off. "That's all I know. Aren't you glad?"

An hour after Bette and Nydia departed, Agatha wasn't surprised when Virgil phoned and asked if he could drop in briefly. She knew he liked her a great deal, not for herself as Mrs. Max Mallowan, but for her celebrity as Agatha Christie. Virgil was a snob about wealth and celebrities. This explained his delight in offering his home to Bette rent free. Virgil's mother, Mabel, had reigned briefly before her death as a queen of some of London's better salons. Invitations to her get-togethers were feverishly sought-after. In the mansion next to Agatha's house, when the Wynn family had still lived under one roof, it was not uncommon to see that Mabel had snared the likes of the fine actor Gerald Du Maurier and his daughters, Daphne and Angela, promising young authors; Noel Coward and Gertrude Lawrence; Winston Churchill and his daughter Sarah, who dreamed of a career in the musical theater and was having an affair with Vic Oliver, a popular orchestra leader. She later married him. There was the Duke of Windsor, long before his infamous liaison with Mrs. Wallis Warfield Simpson, of whom Mabel had said, "Never truckle with a woman whose head is too big for her body." Virgil reveled in the celebrity his mother enjoyed, but Sir Roland was dismayed by it all. These notables came to pay homage to his wife, not to him. His star had already been eclipsed. Once he was shattered when, standing at the main entrance, Lloyd George offered him his coat, mistaking him for a butler.

All this Virgil told Agatha when he arrived, and Agatha wondered if she should offer him a whisky or a coffin. He wanted nothing, just to talk. He told her about Mabel as a roundabout means of explaining himself. "I have always felt you disapproved of me, Agatha. I'm not trying to change your mind. I would prefer you liked me, because I admire you very much, as does all my family, as did my beloved mother."

"Your mother was a fool," Agatha said straight out. "She lived for only two things. Herself and you. When your father in his decline needed her love and understanding, she distanced herself from him while selfishly embracing your celebrity and seeking to flourish in your reflected glory. I still can't understand why she committed suicide."

"Neither could anybody. Solomon Hubbard might have been right. Our family physician." Agatha nodded by way of letting him know she knew. "He said it was a sudden mental trauma causing an agonizing depression that caused her to take the overdose of sleeping draughts. I know she dreaded her encroaching old age."

"She was never terribly sensible." Virgil did not rise to his mother's defense. "I'm sure you were aware of that. The profligacy with which she went through what little fortune your father had left. Those charming but pointless salons of hers, just the purchase price of friendships that were not for sale. The way she pursued the Woolfs and that distasteful Sackville-West woman. Forgive me, Virgil, I have gone too far. I apologize."

"This is why I like you, Agatha. You speak your mind with alacrity, which is one of the many reasons why Max adores you. Agatha"—his hands were folded in his lap—"I'm a dying man."

"Yes, I can see."

"There's nothing to be done for me. There's nothing I want done for me. In my will, I'm not as cruel to my father and my sister and brother as my mother was to them. I'll say nothing further about that. I have so much wealth in that terrible old house."

"You'll be out of it on Friday."

"My spirit will be there. I know it will."

"Why do you despise that house?"

"Because of what it did to my family and what it did to me. It's not been a happy house. That's why the others chose to move after my mother's death. I didn't force them to leave, as has been cruelly rumored; they wanted to go. You know we're still on good terms. I see Anthea daily."

"There's no avoiding her," said Agatha squarely.

"This terrible addiction of hers."

Agatha sat up. "To arsenic?"

Virgil's near-dead eyes came miraculously back to life. "To gambling. Why do you say arsenic?"

Trapped, Agatha gave her dissertation on arsenic and strychnine addiction, hoping to hear an admission from Virgil, but none was forthcoming. What he did tell her she found of equal interest.

"Agatha, Anthea has been heavily in debt to several private clubs. I have paid them off. But she'll be in debt again. I won't be there for her to lean on, poor darling. She'll need advice, as will my father and brother, on the disposition of my private collection. I prevail on you to ask your husband to advise my family."

"I can assure you he will be of a great assistance to them."

"As to a fee . . ."

"Stuff and nonsense. You know Max would never hear of that. He's your friend. He's your father's friend. Is there something else?"

"I'm so awfully tired."

"Why do I think there's something else on your mind?"

She thought he was smiling; she couldn't be sure. "Whatever it is, and if I choose not to tell you, I'm sure you'll pursue it in your own inimitable way."

"If that's an invitation, I accept, and if it's a challenge, I more than accept."

"I wish we had been closer friends. I feel I've missed so much."

"I think you were doing a lot of your digging in inappropriate places. Had it not been for your single-mindedness as an archeologist, you might have gotten to know your father better, your siblings, and the lovely Nydia."

"I suppose it's no use saying I now realize my mother was in the way."

"And by the time she was gone, it was too late to mend fences. Poor Mabel. She even had bad luck with her lovers." She paused. "You're not shocked? You knew about them?"

"There wasn't anything subtle about Mabel." He rose and walked to the door. There he turned and spoke again. "But as God is my witness, I have always loved my father. That's why I followed in his footsteps. But as bad luck would have it, it turned out all wrong."

"Perhaps it was as much his fault as yours. Stubborn old fool. He should be with you on this trip."

"I don't think he thinks I'm going to see Egypt again. He knows I'm dying. They all know." He added almost light-heartedly. "I don't think there isn't anybody who doesn't know I'm dying." Agatha's heart skipped a beat. She knew there was more he wanted to tell her. But he said nothing other than goodbye, and for the first time in the many years that she had known him, she was reluctant to witness his departure. She was hoping he'd tell her who he suspected was killing him, but the damned fool chose to be a gentleman to the bitter end. The door closed. Virgil was gone. She had her work cut out for her, and there would be Nydia Tilson and Bette Davis helping, Santa's little elves. Now to attack that cold leg of lamb in the larder, nice and rare, nice and bloody, the way she liked things to be.

4

SATURDAY MORNING WAS GRIM AND GRAY, as autumnal skies over the United Kingdom are wont to be. In the Wynn mansion, in Bette's bedroom, which was more like a suite, Bette and Nydia sat sipping coffee bitter with too much chicory while Nellie Mamby bustled about unpacking Bette's suitcases and steamer trunk and neatly assigning the contents to closets and dresser drawers.

"I hope I can find things after she's finished," said Bette under her breath.

"Relax and don't worry about it." She looked at her wristwatch. "Virgil is on his way. His steamer left two hours ago. Well, no point in dwelling on Virgil. We'll know the worst soon enough."

"Don't we already know it?" She whispered again, "This coffee's *awful*."

"It's the chicory," confided Nydia.

"Chicory? In coffee? How God-awful. It's a good thing Ruthie's not here. She is chicory's mortal enemy. Chicory, no, but cinnamon, yes."

"To hell with the coffee," said Nydia as she got to her feet. "We've got things to do around here. Inventory, my darling friend, inventory. Agatha insists we catalogue the house from top to bottom as a favor to Max, so he can tell the family how much wealth there is and they can rub their hands together greedily. Assuming Virgil's left the lot to them, and I'm sure he has, if only to assuage a guilty conscience."

"You mean it actually bothers him that he inherited his mother's fortune?"

"Yes, I know it did, because he told me it did. That's why he helps them financially." They were descending the broad and beautiful and lushly carpeted staircase to the library, where they had decided to begin, as Nydia considered it the most cheerful room in the house. "I wish Agatha hadn't been so close-mouthed about Virgil's visit the other night. I don't believe he dropped in just to get Agatha to get Max to help the family assess the inventory. Did he expect Max and Agatha to tag everything the way they do at auctions?"

Bette said knowledgeably, "They don't tag things at auctions, Nydia. They list a floor price and then you bid. They tag things at art galleries, but you can always try to bargain. My God, Nydia, have you never been to an auction?"

"Of course I have. I go frequently. I shall take you to Sotheby's, and quite often. But I never bid."

Bette was wide-eyed with amazement. "Not even for something you want?"

Nydia informed her slyly, "You can rarely bid for the things I want." Bette followed her into the library.

Nydia gasped. Bette stared with mouth agape.

Virgil Wynn was seated at the desk, staring at them. They realized the eyes were lifeless, but still it seemed he was staring at them. His hands, in death, clenched the ends of the arm rests as though caught in the midst of a fatal struggle.

Behind them they heard Agatha saying, "My *specialité*. A body in the library." They turned and stared at her. "The front door was ajar, so I let myself in." She carried an armload of flowers from her garden and, in a small net shopping bag dangling from her arm, apples, a box of salt, and a loaf of bread.

"Oh, Agatha, how cold-blooded!" admonished Bette.

"Why cold-blooded? It's quite obvious he's dead. What's not quite obvious is why is he seated at the desk and not on a steamer bound for Egypt. Take these flowers, Nydia, and dump them someplace. Not too close to the body, or when the police get here they'll think we're being facetious. Or do I mean capricious? Anyway, it'll seem like bad luck. And here, Bette, apples with salt and bread for good luck in this house, and I suppose I'm a little late with *that*."

They hadn't heard Nellie Mamby come into the library and were given quite a turn as she said in a sepulchral voice, "It's the curse!"

Bette said in her famous take-charge voice, "It's not the curse. The man is dead, and I don't believe in curses. Now inform the police, please, and when you're done, you can inform the members of his family."

Agatha had advanced to the corpse and was giving it a professional examination. Nydia said to Bette, "What an unfortunate beginning to your stay here. This hasn't put you off the house, has it?"

"At no rent? Are you nuts?"

They turned their attention to Agatha, who was rubbing her hands together like a yegg about to meet the challenge of a safe. They could hear Nellie Mamby on the phone in the hallway trying to explain the situation to the police. Bette, hands on hips, said sternly to Nydia, whose eyes had teared up, "Now, don't you go to pieces on me, my rock of Gibraltar."

Nydia sniffed and managed a smile. "I can't imagine not ever dining with him again. He was such a wonderful host."

"As I suspected," intoned Agatha. "Every signpost indicates arsenic poisoning."

"Shouldn't you wait for the coroner to examine him?" asked Bette.

Agatha said haughtily, "I'm as good as any coroner. Better,

if the truth be known. And anyway, what do you know about coroners?"

"Darling, when you act for the Warner brothers, you're up to your armpits in coroners. I've even been a corpse for them. In a little stinker called *Fog over Frisco.*"

"Oh, how delicious. It's every symptom of arsenic poisoning. The condition of his fingernails, his sallow, sickly skin."

"He used to be so gorgeously suntanned," reminisced Nydia.

"You'll never see that again," said Bette watching Agatha with fascination.

"Your observation was correct, Nydia," said Agatha.

"Which one?" She wondered why Virgil didn't briefly revive and remonstrate at Agatha's rude poking-about. It was really ghoulish molestation, thought Nydia, something she wouldn't dare voice, not to the formidable Mrs. Mallowan.

"The thinning of his hair." She took a pencil from the desk and lifted a small hairpiece for them to see. "Very artfully plastered to his skull. Poor man, he was vain about himself and his looks."

"They were very good looks," defended Nydia.

"I should poke about in his mouth, but I have no stomach for it," said Agatha. Bette and Nydia looked as though they were repelled by the thought. "Well, the coroner will have to do that on his own. But rest assured, he'll find Virgil's teeth are loose." She straightened up, wincing at a short spasm in her back. "I shudder to think of the amount of poison that's accumulated in his system over the Lord only knows how long a period."

Nellie Mamby rejoined them. "The police are on their way. But none of the family's in. They shall have to learn later!" She began to whimper, and Bette crossed to her, put an arm around her, and attempted to console her.

"My God! What's going on in here?" Anthea had arrived, attired, strangely enough, from head to toe in black.

Bette asked her, "How'd you guess?"

Bewildered, Anthea asked, "What are you talking about?"

"Virgil," said Bette, giving the name a very simple reading.

Then Anthea saw the body. She cried out. Agatha went to her. She took her in her arms and said, "Now, now, my dear, You and your family must have recognized he's been failing for months."

"Yes, yes, but now that it's happened and it's real, it's unthinkable."

Past Nellie Mamby Bette saw arriving from the hall two men she presumed to be Sir Roland Wynn and his son Oscar. Each were carrying flowers. Bette said to Agatha, "This is terribly uncanny. Anthea in black and the men bringing flowers."

Anthea explained coldly, "I'm wearing black because I've been to a memorial for an old school chum who was knocked over by a tram. The flowers are for you, Bette." She introduced her father and her brother, who were deaf to Bette's greeting, so stunned were they by the sight of the dead body.

Agatha took charge. "Bette and Nydia found him a short while ago, just as I arrived. I expect he came back here for something he'd forgotten after dining with you, Roland."

"Yes, that's what he did," said Sir Roland, the voice trembling. "Something about some notes he was working on and wanted to continue working on during the voyage."

"I see no notes on the desk," said Agatha.

Bette suggested that he had probably been stricken before he could find them. Agatha asked Mamby if she hadn't heard Virgil return to the house.

"No, Mrs. Mallowan. I sleep in the back. It's very quiet there." She added for good measure, "I'm a very heavy sleeper."

"You don't look all that heavy to me," commented Agatha.

Anthea and Oscar had their heads together, whispering. Sir Roland had crossed to the desk and seemed transfixed by his dead son. His lips moved, but no words emerged. Finally, they heard him ask, "Agatha, who do you think killed him?"

Agatha and Bette exchanged glances. Agatha said, "You think he was murdered? Why?"

Mamby said, "It's the curse, the curse!"

Sir Roland wheeled on her. "I've survived the so-called curse, and so have Howard Carter and numerous others. You listen too much to the damned wireless!"

Agatha persisted, "Roland, who do you think killed him?"

"I haven't any idea at all! But we managed a private moment last night before he left Fouquet's—that's where we dined— and he said something to the effect that he knew he'd been murdered and he would never see me again, and then some soporific blather about forgiving him for not having been a better son to me." He held his head proudly and for a brief moment Bette thought she recognized what had attracted Mabel to him. "I think he was an excellent son. I was very proud of his considerable achievements and shall say so at his memorial. I know, I know. Everyone suspected I was jealous of how he eclipsed me." Slowly he walked away from the desk to a window overlooking the back garden. "I didn't consider he did that to me, not at all. I was honored by my king for discovering Ramatah. The old girl's served me well. I shall express my feelings more elaborately in my memoirs."

"Oh, good, I'm so glad you've decided to put pen to paper," said Agatha. Bette wondered if he wasn't more likely to use a quill.

"Virgil's death made up my mind for me. It shall be my story and Virgil's story." He moved away from the window. "Agatha, do you think your publisher would be interested?"

What an old scoundrel, thought Bette, and Nydia, who'd been about to speak to her, smiled as though she'd succeeded in reading Bette's mind. They heard Agatha say, "I think he'd be very interested. He's quite partial to antiquity. He publishes me."

"Oh, come!" said Sir Roland. "You're not all that old."

"It's at times like these that I feel all that old." Agatha said. "He's publishing Helen Grosvenor's autobiography." She told Bette and Nydia, "A very strange woman who insists she's the reincarnation of an Egyptian princess, and the man she's been living with for ages now is actually her lover of the ancient days, a mummy brought back to life."

Bette's eyes sparkled. "I saw the movie!"

Agatha was startled. "How can they have made a motion picture of a story that hasn't as yet been published?"

"Well, then she must have seen the picture and stolen the plot. It was called *The Mummy*. He was played by Boris Karloff, and the reincarnated princess was Zita Johann."

Agatha looked beaten. In a small voice she asked, "My dear, may I have one of those apples I brought you?"

"Help yourself."

Brother Oscar spoke up. "I shall compose an oratorio and dedicate it to Virgil. We must share him with the world."

"You do that, Oscar," said Nydia, knowing that if he ever did compose it, he'd be composing it for an audience of one, himself. She confided to Bette, "He's completely atonal. I'm sure he hears sweet music in his head, but somehow, when it's transferred to a blank page, what emerges is a lot of deafening cacophony."

Nellie Mamby hurried to answer the door chimes.

Said Bette, "That must be the police."

Waiting to be admitted into the house, Detective Inspector Howard Cayman said to his assistant, Detective Lloyd Nayland, "The place will be swarming with the press at any moment now. Reporters and photographers trampling over this beautiful lawn. Virgil Wynn isn't exactly some anonymous East End spiv." He smiled. "How quaintly did the housekeeper put it when she phoned in the alarm?"

"Something to the effect that Virgil Wynn, the famed archeologist, has been done in; he's seated at his desk right now stiffer then a walking stick, and his friend Mrs. Mallowan suspects foul play."

"I suspect foul case." He said with a snort, "Mrs. Mallowan suspects foul play indeed. If there's something I won't tolerate when I'm conducting an investigation, it's a busybody of a biddy making unwanted noises." The door opened.

Nellie Mamby asked, "Are you the police?"

"You rang for the police?" Nellie nodded. "Then here we are."

"Mrs. Mallowan says you should also have a coroner." She asked Lloyd Nayland, "Are you the coroner?"

"No, I'm not. Actually, he's hurrying up the path towards us."

Nellie saw a middle-aged man of medium height carrying a medical bag and holding a hand over his bowler to keep it from blowing off his head as a strong wind suddenly lay siege to St. John's Wood. Nellie hadn't the vaguest idea what a coroner was supposed to look like.

Inspector Cayman said somewhat whimsically (and he was frequently given to attacks of whimsy), "He is Mr. Ambrose MacDougal. I am Inspector Cayman. With me is my assistant, whose surname is Nayland. Now that I have seen to the amenities, out of the kindness and generosity of my heart, would you kindly conduct us to the *corpus delicti*, meaning the late Virgil Wynn, so we can set about trying to solve the crime, that is, if a crime has been committed."

"Bloody freezing," muttered Ambrose MacDougal, "and me without my topcoat."

The procession led by Nellie Mamby crossed the main hall to the library, peppered with appropriate and inappropriate comments about the treasures on display. Inspector Cayman admired what he saw. Said Nayland, "It's like a bloody museum!"

"And why not?" questioned Cayman. "We're in the home of a celebrated archeologist."

"Bloody grave robber," muttered Nayland, who was an undercover socialist.

As they entered the library, Sir Roland introduced himself. "The deceased is my son."

"My condolences," said Cayman, who Bette thought

would be more at home as the suave *maître d'* of an exclusive Mayfair restaurant. Cayman introduced himself and his cohorts.

"Ah, yes," said Ambrose MacDougal while doffing his hat and pressing it upon Nellie for safekeeping. "There sits the corpse. So lifelike, don't you think?" Cayman agreed while sotto voce cautioning the coroner against any jocularity, for this seemed an unusually sober bunch.

Cayman looked about the room and decided that the lady taking a last bite of an apple was probably Mrs. Mallowan. He said to her, "Correct me if I'm wrong, but are you Mrs. Mallowan?"

"Clever deduction. Nellie Mamby's probably told you I suspect Virgil's been murdered. We'll get to that in a moment." She introduced the others. Cayman sized up everyone very thoroughly and very professionally. Agatha saved Bette Davis for the last. "And this is the very famous Hollywood star Bette Davis."

Cayman oozed charm. "Miss Davis needs no introduction."

Bette said as she exhaled smoke from her latest cigarette, "She will if you get the bizarre notion that I committed the crime."

"This is quite marvelous," said Cayman. "Everyone's convinced a crime has been committed, which I'm afraid, Ambrose, makes your presence somewhat superfluous."

"No it doesn't," said MacDougal as he poked about the body. "You always need a coroner. Who else will do the autopsy?"

"Possibly, Mrs. Mallowan. Do you do autopsies, madam?"

"Only when invited," snapped Agatha. Then she said quite authoritatively, "The man's been systematically poisoned over an unspecified period of months. Arsenic more than likely. There are all the symptoms."

"She's quite right, Cayman," said the coroner jovially. "She's right on the mark." He said to Agatha, "You're very good, Mrs. Mallowan." He pointed at Virgil. "Classic case. From a superficial examination, I would say he should have been dead weeks ago. Amazing he's lasted this long."

"My brother was always terribly stubborn," said Oscar.

"Oscar!" cried Anthea in admonishment.

"Meaning no disrespect," Oscar defended himself. "I was only stating a fact recognized by all of us."

"Speak for yourself, Oscar," said Bette, thinking it unjust that this ninny shared the name of her prized Academy Award. "I thought Virgil was a charming gentleman."

Anthea said, "You hardly knew him."

Bette said with hooded eyes, "In my bailiwick, I'm considered a very good judge of character."

Cayman made a mental note to avoid locking horns with the actress. She sounded like a woman who didn't suffer fools gladly. "Miss Davis, since you pride yourself on spot judgments, how do I strike you?"

"You? You should be leading a party of four to their reserved table."

Agatha laughed. "I like that, Bette, that's rather good."

"I like it too," said Cayman. "Just as long as you didn't catalogue me as just another flatfoot. That *is* how I'd be referred to in America, isn't it?"

"Only by gangsters and their molls." Bette found herself getting interested in him. "Have you ever been to America, Inspector?"

"Not on my salary. But someday I hope I shall visit."

The coroner said, "There's not much more I can do here. I'll send the boys in with the stretcher." He retrieved his hat and left, after bowing his head in admiration to Agatha. She favored him with a smile of gratitude.

"Ambrose!" called out Cayman. "Tell the others to keep any invaders outside the wall. I'll give them a statement later." He said to the assemblage, "Meaning the press. I'm sure they'll be converging soon, if they're not already here."

"Oh, dear," said Bette, "can you keep my name out of

this?" She explained her upcoming lawsuit and her fear of judicial prejudice.

"I'll do my best," promised Cayman, "but many of the members of our press are brothers to vultures."

"I'd be most appreciative."

Cayman asked, "Is there some other room we can use? The removal of a corpse can be a most unpleasant sight."

Anthea spoke up. "We can use the drawing room."

"Oh, can we?" Bette was lighting another cigarette.

Anthea looked bug-eyed. "Oh, I'm so sorry. I forget the house is yours now."

Bette said with a tight smile, "Temporarily." She blew a smoke ring and then said, "We can use the drawing room." She led the way.

Cayman said to Nayland, "You had an affair with an American. Was she this bossy?"

"Yes, bless her. It's what made her interesting."

When settled in the drawing room, Cayman and Nayland ogled the formidable array of artifacts. "I say," said Cayman. "What a store of loot!"

Sir Roland objected strongly. "This isn't loot. This is the result of scientific investigations. You should respect that." He was ignored and left to bristle inwardly.

Cayman gave his attention to Agatha. "Mrs. Mallowan, poison is supposedly a woman's weapon."

"Supposedly my foot. It most definitely is. I've used it many times."

"I beg your pardon?" Cayman couldn't believe he'd be hearing a confession of guilt this soon.

"In my books. In my plays. In my short stories."

Bette intervened. "Inspector, Mrs. Mallowan is better known under the name Agatha Christie."

"Oh, my, my, and my! I should have recognized you from your dust jackets!" He extended his hand to shake hers. "I'm a great admirer of yours despite the fact that you cheat so much."

"I don't cheat," said Agatha forthrightly. "I think I play fair with my readers. If I cheat anyone it's myself. I set such difficult problems that I often forget how my darlings are supposed to solve them. Damnation, Bette, you left the apples in the library."

"I'll send Mamby to fetch them."

"Oh, don't bother. I eat too bloody many of them anyway. There are dried-up cores all over my house and in the garden. Let's let the authorities get on with their jobs."

"I gather you are subletting this house," Cayman said to Bette.

"Yes. Virgil very generously asked me to occupy the house while he was in Egypt. I hope there will be no objection now. Nydia and I were on our way to catalogue the artifacts this morning, when we found Virgil."

Sir Roland spoke for himself and his children when he assured Bette she was more then welcome to stay. Bette thanked him and then told Cayman that Virgil was to have sailed for Egypt early that morning. Sir Roland told of the previous night's dinner and Virgil's returning to the house for some notes he'd left behind, during which search death unexpectedly overtook him.

Agatha said, "Interesting way of putting it—death unexpectedly overtaking him—when I strongly suspect he'd been ingesting arsenic over an unspecified period of time. Inspector Cayman, are you familiar with arsenic?"

"Not intimately, but we've crossed paths before."

Agatha was delighted to educate him. When she was finished, Cayman asked with incredulity, "How do you know Queen Victoria was addicted to arsenic?"

"And strychnine. It's in several reference books. That sort of addiction was prevalent in her era, but then, it was carefully monitored by a physician, or at least I assume it was. It's still going on today, I'm told, but on a much more isolated scale."

"Mrs. Mallowan, you absolutely astonish me with your

criminal knowledge. I say! You don't happen to know the identity of Jack the Ripper, do you?"

"Not really. I have my theories, as does everyone else. I know only one thing about him for sure: he was sinestral."

"I beg your pardon?"

"Sinestral. Left-handed. That was deduced from how the knife, his weapon, disemboweled his victims."

Bette said with raised eyebrows, "Charming conversation."

Cayman was pacing about with no particular destination in mind. "Death in small doses. Now how might these be administered to him?" He stopped in front of Nellie Mamby. "I assume you're the housekeeper." She nodded. She was not happy. "And I assume you are also the cook."

"Yes, I am." Her hands were clenched tightly together. "I didn't kill him!"

"I haven't said you did. But you cooked for him."

She blurted out, "He's had little appetite for weeks! He couldn't keep food down. I think he as much starved to death as was poisoned the way you claim."

Agatha reassured her warmly, "He was poisoned."

"He's just been eating a little gruel, a little soup . . ."

"Tea and coffee?" interjected Agatha.

"Oh, yes, of course, tea and coffee."

"Milk and sugar for his tea?"

"Oh, yes. Always milk and sugar."

Agatha said, "Inspector, I'm sure I don't have to advise you to have the sugar analyzed."

Bette said, "Nydia and I had coffee earlier. We both take sugar."

"Oh, my God," said Nydia.

"I used the company bowl," said Nellie.

Cayman asked, "And what is the company bowl?"

"The one we use for company," explained Nellie.

"Dug up somewhere?" persisted Cayman.

"Harrod's."

Anthea volunteered, "I used to bring him custards and rice puddings. Oscar used to bring him his favorite soup, cock-a-leekie."

"And I brought him cream buns," said Sir Roland, "among other nasty, gooey desserts he favored. So I suppose we all could have been poisoning him, though I find it a rather ridiculous assumption. I wouldn't know where to acquire a poison of any sort."

Agatha advised him, "It's contained in any variety of weed killer. And weed killers are easily obtainable."

Sir Roland exploded, "I find this entire discussion intolerable! How dare it be insinuated that we killed our son and brother!"

"Sir Roland," said Cayman in a voice that was calm and contained, "no insinuation has been made at all, by either me or Mrs. Mallowan or Miss Davis or Miss Tilson."

"Thanks for remembering me," said Nydia smoothly. "I also contributed to the effort to reawaken Virgil's slumbering appetite. I frequently brought a vegetable stew."

"Lots of mushrooms in them stews!" said Nellie swiftly. "You can't be too careful with mushrooms! There's a lot of poisonous ones out there!"

"Well, if that's the case, Inspector, you should be investigating my greengrocer. I don't know about poisonous mushrooms, but I do suspect he pads my bills mercilessly."

"Dear God," said Cayman, holding a cool hand to his now feverish brow. "Why couldn't the man have been thoughtful enough to drop dead of a heart attack?"

Anthea gasped, "Jokes are uncalled for!"

Cayman replied, "I am not joking, Miss Wynn. I foresee too many complications with this case, and though one always welcomes a simple solution, I do not for once harbor the theory that there is an epidemic of multiple poisoners around here!"

Nellie Mamby's voice was now heard, and it was high-pitched and shrill. "I can tell you this now that Mr. Virgil's dead. He promised I wasn't to tell a soul, and certainly not Miss Bette, since she was moving in."

Bette moved in slowly on Nellie Mamby. "And what is it that I wasn't supposed to be told?"

Outside the sky was darkening and there were flashes of lightning to be seen.

"Well, Mamby, what's the secret?"

"The house is *haunted!*"

There was a tremendous thunderclap that made the windows rattle.

Bette removed a cigarette from her mouth and said, "Perfect timing."

5

Nellie Mamby persisted, against a background of thunder and flashes of lightning. "The house is haunted! The house is cursed!"

Bette felt on the verge of laughter but managed to control herself. "So you insist the house is haunted. And Virgil believed you."

"He didn't disbelieve me." Her eyes darted all over the place nervously.

Bette continued, "Is it haunted by Egyptian spirits or good old home-grown British spirits?"

"All kinds, if you ask me." She said to Sir Roland, "Many times I overheard him conversing with Miss Mabel."

Sir Roland looked incredulous. "Virgil and the shade of my wife conversing?"

"How Shakespearean," commented Agatha, who would have been at a loss had she been asked to identify the play.

Bette said to Nydia, "I'm getting giddy."

Nydia said in a voice that meant business, "You forget, Bette, that I deal with the afterworld. And very successfully."

"I tell you the house is haunted," persisted Nellie Mamby. "I know it is. I told Mr. Virgil I was hearing strange noises coming from the basement in the dead of night."

Cayman was getting interested. "Can you describe these noises?"

"They sounded like digging noises. The first time I told Mr. Virgil he said it was stuff and nonsense. But I know what I heard, and what I heard was the sound of digging. I could hear it clearly because my quarters are directly over that part of the basement."

Asked Cayman, "Did Mr. Wynn investigate?"

"I don't think so. If he did, it was when I wasn't about. Maybe when I was out shopping or on my day off, which is Thursday. That's when I visit my sister, who lives in Twickenham."

Bette knew there was a movie studio in Twickenham, one of London's suburbs. It was where Ludovico Toeplitz was planning to film *I'll Take the Low Road.*

Cayman asked Nellie, "Have you yourself gone down to investigate?"

"*Me?* Are you daft? Me go down there alone? I haven't been down there since before Miss Mabel died. She was down there all the time poking around the jewelry and them things she called curios." She added hoarsely, "There's bodies down there."

"Bodies? Corpses?" Cayman was astonished.

Sir Roland explained, "There are a few mummies stored in the basement. We assumed they were household slaves. Slaves were frequently entombed with their masters. It was the custom. What's down there is the stuff Virgil wanted for his museum." He elucidated, "Virgil's dream was to construct a private museum to bear our name and to perpetuate our accomplishments, 'The Wynn Museum of Archeology.' Lord knows he had the wherewithal. Mabel was a very wealthy woman. She left the lion's share to Virgil so he could finance his own expeditions."

"She left it to him out of sheer spite," snapped Anthea, startling Bette, who was glad to know the mouse could roar.

"Anthea! Keep quiet!" commanded Sir Roland.

"I will not keep quiet. I'm fed up with keeping quiet. I think I shall write my own book, one that will tell the truth! She and Virgil were cut from the same cloth. Selfish and spiteful."

Nydia joined in, "He was very generous to you! He paid your gambling debts."

"He was overtaken by guilt when he began to realize he wasn't long for this world. He was well aware he couldn't take it with him!"

Bette suggested, "He might have tried. Constance Bennett says, if she can't take it with her, she won't go. And believe you me, this is the one Bennett with whom nobody trifles."

"I suppose now dear Virgil is to be sanctified. A martyr. That's a laugh!"

"Enough, Anthea, enough!" Sir Roland was at the liquor cabinet in search of comfort. The rain was pelting against the windows and Detective Nayland was feeling a bit sorry for the press corps, who by now he was sure were huddled outside the wall. Nayland heard Cayman speaking to him.

"Lloyd, have a look in the basement." He asked Nellie Mamby, "Is there a torch handy?"

"He doesn't need one. There's a switch just inside the basement door. It floods the place with light."

"There are so many doors. Where exactly will I find the one that leads to the basement?"

"It's in the hall outside the kitchen. I'll show you." Nayland dutifully followed the housekeeper, who was chattering away about ghosts and spirits and things that go dig in the night, while Bette was thinking, If this were a scene in a play, Mamby's departure would have gotten her a round of applause. Instead she was rewarded with a clap of thunder.

Anthea accepted an unrequested glass of sherry from her father. Oscar helped himself to one while Bette concluded that selfishness was a family trait, as no one else was offered any refreshment. Agatha spoke up briskly, "I'll have one too, if you don't mind?" She smiled to Cayman and her two girlfriends. "Anyone else?" Everybody else said yes, and Oscar busied himself.

There was a lot on Cayman's plate. Virgil had been poisoned and five suspects had had the opportunity to do him in or to help his departure along. He felt someone's eyes boring into his person and when he turned to look he saw it was Agatha. "Yes?"

"I was wondering, Inspector. You won't forget to have the contents of his medicine chest analyzed?"

"Certainly not. One doesn't graduate from the police academy without analyzing the contents of a medicine chest. But all things in due time. As a fellow sleuth, you certainly recognize that I'm plunged into the midst of a murder case that has many ramifications and mystifications and a wide variety of cations and a very tangled skein of emotions, some of which I suspect have yet to surface." He took her by the arm and led her to a part of the room where he felt assured they would not be overheard. It didn't escape him that Bette looked tempted to follow and join them but apparently decided to wait for an invitation, which would not be forthcoming. Instead she busied herself with wondering about Nydia's withdrawal into some heavy preoccupation.

Cayman was confiding to Agatha, "That sudden outburst from Anthea, it seems to me, has been a long time simmering."

"Indeed. I suspect there's a lot more material for outbursts waiting to erupt. Um, Sir Roland's lovely eulogy to his son was nicely worded for an impromptu rendition, but I buy none of it. His green envy of Virgil will never ripen for plucking. I strongly suspect the old boy holds no brief for any of his offspring. Then there's Mabel, his late unlamented. He despised her. You, of course, have heard of her salons."

"If I may say so, to the extreme point of utter boredom."

"Utter boredom," echoed Agatha. "You make it sound like a province in India."

"Mrs. Mallowan, I consider whimsy my private territory."

Agatha said solemnly, "I shall remember never again to trespass. Now, if I may get back on the track. Mabel's affairs were notorious. There is one lie I would like to lay to rest. Mabel did not clean out Sir Roland's coffers. She didn't need his money. She had, as you must by now have gathered, tons of her own. Roland did himself in financially. Wild speculations in the stock market to try to increase the modest wealth he accomplished as a lecturer and occasional wireless speaker, and by bootlegging artifacts. But unfortunately, he wasn't clever. So, in my books, Sir Roland remains what he has been for many years now, an embittered has-been."

"What about Anthea? I thought she adored brother Virgil."

"She was always underfoot, waiting on him, doing his errands, in general making a sycophantic fool of herself. Contrary to what you've heard so far, Mabel did leave the others something. I know because she consulted me and I convinced her a little something would help sweeten their sour memories of her. So that's what she left them. A little something. Sir Roland's disappeared trying to finance an expedition to do some digging in Iceland. There are fossils to be found in Iceland. I'm not particularly interested, but my husband says they're positively there. You know my husband is quite an eminent archeologist?"

"I do indeed."

"Max has tried to help Roland, but the fool—Roland, not Max—has accumulated too many enemies. Anthea gambled away all of what she received. I pity her. She's very lonely, and she'll be lonelier still without Virgil. She writes verse. Blank verse. Terribly blank verse."

"Not very good?"

"As I'm frequently given to advising, 'Without rhyme, there's no reason.' "

"And where does this leave brother Oscar?"

"In the background, where he's always been and where he belongs."

"If Nellie Mamby had it in for Virgil, she deserves full marks for sticking around for what I assume were a good many years."

"She gets a very good wage. She has a lovely suite of rooms in the back of the house. She handles the household money and you can draw your own conclusions as to what's been happening there. Now, Inspector, let me lead you down another path, which I'm sure you realize exists. The house is cluttered with uncatalogued artifacts. The basement is a treasure house. There is much more in the attics. I have long suspected that every so often Nellie and the family have been helping themselves to a relic or two and traded them to dealers. I'm sure Virgil knew this too, but I must repeat, whatever one says about Virgil, praiseful or disparaging, this above all: he was always the perfect gentleman, and perfect gentlemen don't accuse their relatives or the hired help of criminal pilfering. I might add that a lot of Mabel's hoarding was thanks to her excellent eye for the valuable."

"Where do you put Nydia Tilson and her vegetable stew?"

"I put Nydia in my reception room and her stew in my stomach. We're very old friends. We've known each other for years. Surely you know her reputation as a brilliant medium."

"Ah! Shame on me. She's *that* Nydia Tilson!"

"How many Nydia Tilsons are there?"

Cayman wigwagged a finger under her nose. "You're trespassing."

"That will never do. Sorry. Nydia and Virgil were lovers for a time. She rejected him as a husband, however, and I think she nurses a regret there. Nydia has a very warm heart and a sunny disposition, and is a very friend indeed when you desperately need one, but I think that all her life to date, the way Diogenes sought his honest man, Nydia has held her lamp high in search of *la grande passion*, though she has yet to find it."

"How many of us do?"

Nellie Mamby returned to the room and asked Bette if everyone was staying for lunch. "I hope not," she said quickly and sincerely.

"I've stocked the larder for the weekend, but there's not enough for this lot, and Saturday the shops close early. What shall I do?"

"Do nothing, and I'm sure the Wynns will take the hint and go about their business elsewhere, unless"—she added with relish—"the inspector decides to haul them back to Scotland Yard and grill them."

"I beg your pardon? Grill them? How?"

"Sorry, Mamby. That's American slang for the third degree." Mamby remained nonplussed. "Cross-examine them. Question them."

Mamby was frightened. "Me too?"

"Have you something to hide?"

Mamby said, suddenly sagacious, "Haven't we all?"

"Nydia?" Agatha called out sharply as she and the inspector rejoined the others. "Nydia?"

Nydia was aroused from a reverie. "What? What is it?"

"My dear, your face is a study! What's bothering you?"

"A séance. Agatha, I think a séance is definitely called for."

Bette chimed in, "You mean to try to contact Virgil, to ask him to name his murderer?" She almost said "name his poison" and was glad she hadn't.

"Oh, what a marvelous idea!" she said to the others. "I love séances. They always raise my spirits."

In the basement, Lloyd Nayland was awestruck. He wished he had a flashbulb camera to record the riches spread out before him. He took in stride the mummies he came across, but the jewelry, the gem-studded artifacts, the magnificent vases and urns and tapestries dazzled him. He wandered among the riches with a dazed expression on his face until he came across something that sobered him.

What seemed to be a shallow grave was dug in the floor. There was a pick and a shovel lying alongside it. Nellie Mamby's ghosts. He hastened back to the drawing room, entered, and thought he was hearing plans to hold a séance in the Wynn library later that night. He didn't as yet try to catch Cayman's eye. He wanted to hear more about the séance.

"The library is perfect," said Nydia. "It's where he died and he still might be hovering." Bette suppressed a shiver. She hoped he wasn't thinking of paying her a visit later that night after the others had gone.

Sir Roland scoffed, "I don't believe in any of this mumbo jumbo!"

"Be still, Roland," commanded Agatha. "The London Society of Spiritualists is a very formidable organization, and Nydia's a member in very good standing."

Chin high, Nydia said, "Sir Arthur Conan Doyle was a strong believer in spiritualism."

"Was he indeed? Has anyone heard from him lately?" asked Sir Roland with a slight sneer in his voice.

"I knew Sir Arthur," said Agatha. "He was never very communicative." As far as she was concerned, that settled the question of the creator of Sherlock Holmes. "Shall we say eight o'clock sharp? And I think everyone in this room should participate. Don't you agree, Inspector?"

"Absolutely. Eight o'clock sharp."

Bette was standing next to him. "You're really taking this seriously, aren't you?"

"Miss Davis—may I call you Bette, by the way?"

"Since you so charmingly emphasize the 'tee' in 'Bette,' you most certainly may. But I shall continue to call you 'Inspector.' What was that given name of yours again?"

"Howard, as in Leslie Howard."

"Did two pictures with him. He always tries to get his

leading ladies into the sack. He laid claim to a fair percentage of success, though 'laid claim' is an unintended pun. But you were beginning to say . . ."

"In a murder investigation, before you can lead the suspects into areas of self-revelation, it is often wise to let them first attempt to lead you. I have nailed murderers under some of the most unlikely circumstances."

"And so the séance might be both amusing and revealing."

"What I'm really doing is following Miss Christie's lead. She's a very clever woman, and I know she might be on to something but keeping it to herself until she's ready to spring it. You have the most remarkable eyes, Bette."

"I'm often told that. Where I come from they call them 'popeyes.'"

"You mean like that cartoon creature, the sailor?"

"No, I mean eyes that are about to pop out. *Ouch!*" Sir Roland had brushed past her on his way back to the liquor cabinet.

"What is it?" asked Cayman.

"I do believe Sir Roland pinched me!"

"Why, the old rake!"

"Mother warned me there'd be knights like this."

Nayland joined them. He told Cayman what he had found in the basement in addition to the wealth.

"A grave?" Bette's eyes were indeed popping. "That explains Mamby's ghosts, doesn't it?"

"It does indeed," said Cayman. "Now, who do you suppose would be digging down there in the middle of the night?"

Bette cried out to Agatha, "Mr. Nayland's found a grave in the basement!" She heard something from Nellie Mamby that sounded like a strangled shriek.

"How marvelous!" said Agatha.

"It's a shallow grave," explained Nayland.

"Mr. Nayland," said Agatha, "a grave is a grave. And shallow or deep, its existence in the basement of a residence should be considered highly suspect."

70

Bette said eagerly, "Let's go see for ourselves!"

A few minutes later, all save Nellie Mamby had descended to the basement. Agatha and Bette were goggle-eyed at the sight of the treasures. Nydia had been there before at Virgil's invitation to inspect it, and it was certainly nothing new to the members of the Wynn family. Nayland led the way to the grave.

Bette said, "I guess it's a grave. Doesn't look big enough to me to hold a coffin."

"I don't think it was meant for a coffin," said Cayman. "I think there's something already buried down there."

"A body?" Agatha looked bloodthirsty, or at least Bette thought she did.

Sir Roland told them, "I think there are other artifacts buried down there. Virgil must have become overcome with guilt and remorse, and decided, before death claimed him, to share them with his partner."

"And who might that be?" asked Cayman.

"Myself." He sighed. "When Virgil set out on his first expedition in search of the first Ptolemy king, I was able to help finance him. Everyone thought it was Mabel, but it was not; it was me. Mabel didn't want another archeologist in the family." He paused, then quickly continued, "She thought one was tiresome enough."

Poor bastard, thought Bette.

Sir Roland was speaking with difficulty. "Virgil brought back much of this lot"—he made a sweeping gesture with his hand—"adding others from subsequent digs. Our deal was that he was to share the profits with me. But I soon suspected he was holding out. There was a Ptolemy grail one of his assistants told me he had uncovered, worth hundreds of thousands of pounds. But I never saw it." He now sounded deeply wounded by this memory. "There was a lot I never saw. I think it's buried under the basement floor. And it pains me to think that Mabel knew of this hidden treasure and that's where most of her own wealth originated." He said to Anthea and Oscar. "Your mother was not a very nice person!" He turned and walked away from the group.

"Anthea," said Oscar, "do you realize we can lay claim to a great deal of this loot?"

Agatha offered some wise counsel. "I suggest you wait until Virgil's solicitors make public his final instructions. You may find that, as your father has suggested, he had legally made amends to atone for his perfidy, if indeed a perfidy was perpetrated."

Anthea asked Agatha, "You think Father's been fabricating?"

"I think it's too soon to draw any conclusions. Don't you agree, Inspector?"

"This basement puts me in mind of a Christmas pantomime."

Agatha gave way to impatience. "Inspector, this is hardly the time or the place for non sequiturs."

Cayman was amused. "I'm afraid I did not intend my remark as such. It was an honest observation."

"Do you plan to assign someone to dig further into this grave?"

"Oh, dig we must." He was enjoying sparring with the author. He liked her feistiness and her charming sense of humor. It interested him to see the way she seemed to go out of her way to defer to others, the way she held her tongue long enough to let Nydia Tilson or Bette Davis make an observation. And her patience with him was highly admirable. Whereas he was slow and methodical, she liked to swoop down and pounce. The medicine chest. The grave. The séance. No second thoughts about any of them. He wasn't too deep in thought not to notice the way Anthea and Oscar were examining the display of valuable curios, the hunger on their faces. Poor sods. And there's Bette lighting up another cigarette and the Tilson woman joining her.

The séance. He'd attended several in the course of his profession, all patently phony. Yet he'd enjoyed them. He remembered one at which a participant fainted upon hearing his wife calling to him. Seems the woman was not yet dead. He recalled carting at least three so-called mediums to jail on charges of jiggery-pokery. He was positive he saw no such fate awaiting Nydia Tilson. He trusted Agatha's judgment. Then he realized Sir Roland was no longer with them. Anthea suggested he'd returned upstairs, to the comfort of the liquor cabinet. Cayman suggested they all return to the drawing room.

They found Sir Roland standing with his back to the blazing fire that Nellie Mamby had undoubtedly decided to kindle now that there was no longer the threat that Virgil would chide her. Sir Roland was warming a snifter of brandy between the palms of his hands. He was staring out the window on his right. The rain was abating. Cayman deputized Nayland to attend to the press, whose anxiety, despite the rain, he was sure had not dampened. Anthea and Oscar had luncheon appointments and were anxious to be on their way. Nydia reminded them the séance would start promptly at eight. They offered their father a lift, but he was in no hurry to leave. Bette gave a sigh of relief at their departure and hoped Sir Roland would soon follow suit.

Bette took Nydia by the arm and led her to another corner of the room. "See what you can do about sending the old boy on his way. I'll have Mamby prepare some lunch for us."

"I must be on my way too," said Agatha. "I have a chapter of my new novel in the typewriter and I'd like to finish it before dinner. Bette, Nydia." She lowered her voice conspiratorially. "Why not join me for a spot of dinner at six?" They were delighted by the invitation. "I'll do something simple, like toad-in-the-hole. Bette, your cheeks have suddenly lost color. It's simply pork sausages in a circle of mashed potatoes. Quite nourishing and quite filling. Or would you prefer bubble-and-squeak?"

Gad, pondered Bette, will the British and the Americans ever speak the same language? "Pig-in-your-hole sounds just great." Agatha didn't correct her.

Agatha said to Cayman, "I must say, you're unlike any detective I've ever written. You're so charmingly urbane."

"How very kind of you." He was tempted to add "And no detective you've ever written bears any resemblance to any detective I have known," but that might have led to a debate for which at the moment he had no stomach.

"Roland, you're much too close to the fire," warned Agatha. "We can't have you immolated, now. I'm sure the inspector has so many more questions to ask you." With a quick wave of her hand to no one in particular she departed. Bette instructed Mamby to put a lunch together for herself, and Nydia then, out of politeness, as he made no move to go, asked Sir Roland if he cared to join them.

"No, no thank you. I always dine at my club on Saturdays, myself and the other living artifacts."

"You're much too hard on yourself," Bette said.

"I'm an old fogy, my dear Miss Davis, but not an old fool. I'm lunching with Howard Carter, you know, who found King Tut's tomb. He's been very depressed lately. I shall cheer him up immeasurably when I tell him Virgil is dead. See you all at eight." On his way out he handed his empty snifter to Cayman, who rewarded the old man with a stiff bow from the waist. Bette retrieved the snifter and placed it on a table with the other abandoned glasses.

"Care to lunch with us, Inspector?"

"How polite of you to ask. But I must rescue Nayland from the press, and we must get back to the Yard and put in a hard afternoon's work. By the way, Bette, will you please emphasize to Miss Mamby that she's not to touch anything in Virgil's medicine cabinet?"

"Supposing she already has?"

"If so, she won't admit it."

"Where I come from, they cast stones. Here they cast suspicions."

"Have you ever been involved in a murder case before?"

"No, I haven't. I feel quite privileged to be mixed up in this one, even if only indirectly."

He smiled. "I find you terribly direct. With which I shall depart. See both you charming ladies at eight. By the way, Miss Tilson, I hope you don't think I've been ignoring you."

She said smartly, "I'm not easily ignored."

"No. Of course not. There's so much I want to learn about Virgil Wynn that I'm sure I'll never learn from the family."

"I'll do my best to live up to your expectations." She smiled superficially. "Until tonight."

After he was out of earshot, Nydia said to Bette, "Has he been flirting with you?"

"I haven't noticed."

"When he introduced himself I recognized the name and recalled the rumors about his reputation. He is said to have quite a way with women. There was a scandal about him and some woman suspected of murdering her children. She was proven guilty and they hanged her, and if I remember correctly, her husband accused Cayman of getting her confession while under the bedcovers."

"Why, the clever beast! Well, I like him. I like the way he handles his suspects. Anyway, it would be a pity to let all that charm go to waste." The phone rang. "I hope it's my mother. I cabled her the number and this address yesterday." The phone rang again as she asked Nydia to tell Mamby she'd answer it. Nydia hurried out and Bette picked up the phone, which was on a stand next to an easy chair.

"Hello? Yes, operator, this is she. Of course I want to talk to her. She's my mother." She waited patiently for the operator to put her mother through. Then she exclaimed, "Ruthie? You don't sound like you at all. You're so far away. I can barely hear you." She waited. "Oh, that's much better. I'm

75

fine. But darling, you will positively *plotz* when I tell you what I'm mixed up in. *Murder!* My new best friend, Nydia Tilson, and I found a body in the library this morning! No, dear, it wasn't something my host forgot to pack. *He* was the corpse! Poisoned." She elaborated on everything she knew and how exciting it all was, and said yes, the police were keeping her name out of the newspapers. Nydia tiptoed back into the room and sat across from Bette, who was pantomiming a desperate desire for a cigarette. Nydia gave her one and put one in her own mouth, and soon both were puffing away like steam engines gone berserk.

Now Bette sounded exasperated. "Please, Mother, stop insisting! The butler couldn't possibly have done it!" She listened. "For crying out loud, Ruthie, I don't *have* a butler. I have a cook-housekeeper. I don't know yet if she's a treasure, I moved in only this morning. But Ruthie, there *is* treasure!" As Bette babbled away about the basement filled with artifacts and had not yet gotten to the shallow grave, Nydia looked around for a magazine. She could foretell that this conversation was going to be a long one. She found an *Illustrated News* in a rack of magazines next to the fireplace, probably put there by Mamby to help kindle the fires.

She heard Bette saying, "Now, Ruthie, as I said in the cable, it's all over between Ham and myself. You better phone Louella Parsons and give it to her right away or she'll get nastier about me and the trial. Ruthie, I know what I'm doing. There's no changing my mind." Her mother should know by now that her daughter rarely changed her mind. Bette's voice softened. "I expect Ham will be around looking for one of your shoulders to cry on." Her voice hardened. "You two were always conspiring against me! You always took his part against me!" Nydia looked for smoke to come rushing out of Bette's nostrils but was in for a disappointment. Bette was crossing and uncrossing her legs, and Nydia had the good sense to light another cigarette for the actress in tandem with another cigarette for herself. Nydia then crossed to her grateful friend and placed the cigarette between her lips. Bette recognized the possibilities of two cigarettes being lighted by one person. It could be terribly romantic if it were done by a leading man.

"Ruthie, you're getting shrill! You know I can't stand it when you get shrill! You sound like Patsy Kelly and you know I can't stand Patsy Kelly!" Nydia thought she recognized the name, some movie comedienne or another. "All right, Ruthie. Calm down. I'm sorry if I've gotten you upset. Kindly remember I'm a stranger in a strange land where they barely speak our language! You know what they call hard candy? Boiled sweets! And I'm invited to dinner tonight at my neighbor's home and she offered me a choice of something called toad-in-the-hole—" Nydia held the open magazine close to her face to camouflage her rising hysteria—"or something called bubble-and-squeak." Pause. "No, Ruthie! Not Buck and Bubbles! They're that marvelous Negro song-and-dance team. Oh, Ruthie! Don't make a federal case out of it! I'm not shouting!" she shouted. "Ruthie! Hang up!" She calmed down as she listened to the urgency in her mother's voice. "All right, Ruthie, cut the histrionics. I promise I won't get myself murdered. My neighbor says she predicts a very long life for me. Well, she ought to know, she's killed enough people!" Nydia could contain herself no longer and exploded with laughter. "Ruthie, you've got it all wrong. She's a famous writer of murder mysteries; that's where she's killed them. Her name's Agatha Christie." Her eyes widened with amazement. "Nydia! My mother's heard of Agatha! She's read her books. She says she's good!"

Nydia said, "She's not only good, she's wealthy." As an afterthought she added, "Wealth is so comforting." She realized she was talking to herself. Bette was ordering her mother to give her regards to her sister but not to her sister's husband, whom she couldn't tolerate, and to be sure to kiss her dog and tell him to be a good little boy.

The conversation was over and Bette was dabbing at her eyes with a handkerchief. "Sorry."

"No need to apologize. My mother always leaves me in tears. Don't all mothers?"

"You don't understand, Nydia. I absolutely adore my mother. She's my best friend. She encouraged me to act. She brought us up single-handedly. She made so many sacrifices. My father abandoned us when I was eight years old, and *that,* I don't mind telling you, was eighteen years ago." She destroyed the cigarette in an ashtray and stood up. "Oh, the hell with sentiment. Let's go eat."

"We can't until Mamby announces that lunch is ready to be served."

"Oh, for crying out loud!"

Nydia put the magazine aside. "My dear Miss Davis, although we have a history of brutal and fiendish and ghastly murders, there's one thing in this country that will never die."

From the doorway, Mamby announced gravely, "Lunch is ready."

"Tradition!"

6

It was hard to believe that the three women walking in Agatha Christie's beautiful garden behind her town house were involved, if indirectly, in a rather nasty murder. Agatha was reeling off in Latin the names of her wide variety of flowers and greenery, which she proudly claimed to have planted herself. In addition to a green thumb she had a green tongue. When they came to several rows of potted plants, Bette exclaimed, "Oh, how clever! Those *are* pith helmets in which those plants are potted."

"They are indeed," said Agatha. "Army surplus. I found them in the Army and Navy Stores near Victoria Station."

"Now I'm jealous," said Bette, "I wish I had a pith to pot in."

"I've loads more in the potting shed," said Agatha. "Nydia! There you go again, immersed in a purple fog." She was guiding them back to the house. "Certainly the séance isn't worrying you."

"I was thinking about Virgil's family. They were more concerned with their luncheon engagements than they were with the disposal of their brother's body."

Bette's eyes widened again. "I took it as another example of British reserve. I assumed the family lawyer would look after everything pertaining to Virgil's burial." She snapped her fingers. "Say! Do you suppose he might have left instructions to embalm and entomb him? Wouldn't it be marvelous if he had?"

"My dear Bette," said Nydia with exaggerated patience, "there were several limitations to Virgil Wynn. Chief among them was imagination." She said to Agatha, "Actually, I might suggest it to Sir Roland."

"I wouldn't if I were you," said Agatha. "I've known Roland a good many years, and I can positively tell you he doesn't put much store in frivolity."

Later, seated around Agatha's dinner table eating large portions of toad-in-the-hole and sipping an excellent claret, they continued discussing Virgil's survivors. Bette asked Agatha, "Is it really possible one of them is a murderer? Not one of them strikes me as having the disposition for it."

"My dear Bette, there's a bit of a murderer in all of us. We've all flown into rages about someone at one time or another, threatening to kill. Haven't you?"

"My favorite pastime is planning Jack Warner's death."

"There you go. I came close to murdering Mr. Christie but instead wisely chose to disappear for a while, and I calmed down."

"You British are so much better at murder than we Americans. There's very little premeditation in America, it seems to me. It mostly seems to be spur-of-the-moment jobs. Sudden rages that erupt into murder."

Agatha agreed, "We British are so neat and orderly. We plan our murders the way we plan our dinner menus and seating arrangements, with great care and thought."

"What was that theory about poison being almost exclusively a woman's weapon?"

"A myth propagated by men. A vast exaggeration. The Borgia men and the de' Medici men were celebrated poisoners. And our own Richard the Third was suspected on several occasions of administering same. But of course there are suspicions that he's been cruelly slandered because he was deformed, and back then deformity was synonymous with evil." She sipped some wine and then smiled. "What's so wonderful about poison is that there is such a wide variety to choose from. There's the banal and the commonplace, such as rat poison and weed killer, that sort of uninspired thinking. Then there's the exalted and the exotic, such as the many forms of nightshade, curare, inee, nightbane, and so many others I admire and respect and utilize frequently. Of course the more familiar, such as arsenic and strychnine, will always be with us, as well they should, since they have served us so efficiently."

Bette asked, "Why do you suppose Virgil was so slow in dying?"

"Death in small doses, my dear, death in small doses. A gradual fading-away as opposed to instant death. There's less reason for suspicion. You must also remember that so few people can recognize the effects of poisons. We professionals know what to look for. Discoloration of the fingernails I found hard to detect with Virgil, inasmuch as his fingers were manicured periodically, but there was his hair falling out and his teeth loosening, the loss of appetite . . ." Bette pushed her plate away. "So much with Virgil was familiar. Tell me, Nydia. You were very close to Virgil. Did he ever express any suspicions about himself? Did he fear for his life?"

Nydia thought for a few moments. "Like all archeologists, he'd been threatened for despoiling and plundering graves. When out on a dig there were several occasions when his group was stricken with food poisoning, and Virgil often wondered if their food had been doctored."

"Despoiling and plundering. How melodramatic," said Bette.

"There's much melodrama in the profession, as you've already learned, much envy and jealousy, and to judge from Virgil and his father, much illicit goings-on behind the scenes. I am grateful my Max has never been tempted in that direction. I see archeology through Max's eyes. He's driven by a thirst for knowledge about the ancient world, for enlightenment, and by what I consider a very healthy curiosity. He's most fascinated by the ancient Egyptians, the Copts especially."

Bette's face brightened. "Agatha!"

"Yes, dear?"

"Hasn't it ever occurred to you to write a book about the origins of archeology? Possibly a collaboration with your husband? I have a splendid title to suggest!"

"Oh, good! I'm always hard put for titles."

"Where does *Copts and Robbers* strike you?"

"Thankfully, nowhere fatal. Actually, I've notes somewhere for a thriller to be set in Egypt, but I haven't the vaguest idea what I've done with them."

Nydia spoke up. "Maybe they're cached away somewhere with Virgil's missing notes."

Bette said smartly, "I don't think those notes exist. I think it was an excuse of Virgil's to get away from what I suspect was a very boring dinner party and to get back to the house for one final night of work on the grave."

Agatha clapped her hands together. "Two great minds! I've been thinking the same thing! If the notes do exist, notes about what? Instructions for his tailor? A suggestion to his accountant on how to continue swindling the Inland Revenue?" She enlightened Bette. "You call it income tax."

"I call it more than that," said Bette.

"Of course," said Agatha, "we've no real cause to dismiss the existence of the notes so offhandedly. But still, I have a little suspicion in the back of my head that Virgil's murder is not as complicated as we're making it out to be. You know, I might set my book in the ancient home of an Egyptian family much like the Wynns. But my family, of course, will be an exotic one. Royalty, Pharoahs. Princesses and princes. Dark deeds and even darker protagonists."

"I'm looking forward to that one," said Bette enthusiastically.

"I thought you didn't read mysteries."

Bette rounded on Nydia. "That's not exactly true. I read Dashiell Hammett's *The Maltese Falcon.*

"Isn't that a splendid book and isn't he a splendid writer!" Agatha added, "He's in a class by himself."

Bette told her, "I just did the second version of *The Maltese Falcon.* It's been retitled *Satan Met a Lady.*"

"Not very good title," said Agatha.

"Not very good film," countered Bette. "It's one of the reasons I'm fighting for my freedom. The script was so arch and ridiculous."

"But I for one shall look forward to seeing it. What about you, Nydia?"

"I wouldn't miss it for the world."

"Let's watch out for it and we'll go together."

Bette smiled. "You're both too nice."

Agatha was clearing the table. "At times, I suppose I'm nice. Such a weak, simpering word, but I suppose very often *le mot just.*"

Bette said, "It's getting close on eight. Hadn't we better get back to my place? I'll get Mamby to do coffee."

"Excellent idea," said Agatha. "I'll leave everything and clean up in the morning." She asked as they headed out of her house, "Now, the truth, Bette. How did you enjoy the toad-in-the-hole?"

"Why, I thought it was absolutely tasty. I must do a New England boiled for you very soon."

"And what does that consist of?"

"Oh, there's boiled beef, potatoes, carrots, turnips, and if the mood strikes me, some cabbage."

" 'New England boiled,' you call it? Sounds to me more Irish, like corned beef and cabbage!"

"Ha ha ha ha ha. There's a hell of an Irish population in New England! They practically rule Boston!"

Mamby gasped as Bette entered her kitchen.

"Something wrong, Mamby? Is my slip showing?"

"No, Miss Bette. It's just that nobody . . . um . . ."

"Oh, of course! The queen is not in the parlor; the queen is in the kitchen." She dug her hands into the pocket of her skirt, and in a gesture familiar to her audiences, she slowly paced back and forth with her head cocked to one side, much like Charles Laughton posed as Captain Bligh in *Mutiny on the Bounty*. And like the infamous captain, Bette was determined to run a tight ship, if only out of deference to her late host's wishes. "Mamby, we must set something straight at once. Virgil had nothing but praise for you, and I appreciate that. But Mr. Wynn was a man who, I suspect, could do very little for himself."

"He was near-hopeless domestically."

"Of course," said Bette. "A mere man. What do men know about a kitchen?" She knew a lot of men knew a hell of a lot more than either one of them about the running of a kitchen, but she was not about to let Mamby in on her secret.

"So, Mamby, it's going to take a bit of adjusting to each other, and then we shall get on swimmingly."

"I don't know how to swim, ma'am."

There was an edge to Bette's voice. "Then let me do the swimming for both of us. Mamby, much as I enjoy being waited on, the way any normal person would, there are times when I prefer to do for myself. I'm considered quite a good cook. I was taught by an expert. My mother. Our specialties are dishes peculiar to New Englanders. We excel at them. And there will be times, Mamby, when I will tell you I plan to cook dinner for a few guests. I would most certainly appreciate your help. But on the other hand, if the invasion of this territory is too painful for you, I'll understand your repairing to your room to read or knit or play patience or whatever, until such time as I would expect you to serve my guests. I even hope you'll enjoy my cooking as I'm sure I'm going to enjoy yours. If there is a serious problem, let's discuss it tomorrow, as I don't wish to keep my guests waiting and we'll soon be joined by five others. Miss Tilson is conducting a séance," she said brightly.

"One of those spooky things again? She's done them here before. They can be very unpleasant."

"So can life. And now, dear, could you do us a pot of coffee?"

"Right away." Mamby was at a cupboard getting a large coffeepot.

Bette remembered something. "And oh, Mamby, I believe Inspector Cayman suffers from several severe allergies. One of them is an allergy to chicory."

"Indeed?"

"Indeed. There isn't some cinnamon on the premises, by any chance?"

"I think there is."

Bette smiled. "Then why not use some?"

"Yes, Miss Bette." Bette turned to leave. "Oh, Miss Bette?" Bette stopped in her tracks. "Yes?"

"There'll be no need to discuss the kitchen situation tomorrow."

"Oh?"

"I quite understand, if I might say so, woman to woman."

"Oh, good!"

"It's just that when I first started work here and came back after my day off, the kitchen looked as though a bomb had struck it. As gently as I could, I banned Mr. Wynn from the kitchen, and he was amenable."

"Or else he'd have starved to death."

"Oh, you *are* funny!"

After Bette departed, Mamby stood rooted to the floor, tightly clutching the coffeepot. If looks could truly kill, Bette Davis would have had a tragically short career.

While Bette was confronting Mamby in the kitchen, Agatha and Nydia were preparing the beautifully built round table in the library for the séance. They set chairs in place, and Nydia saw to it that there were ashtrays on the table. She also kept glancing at the chair behind the desk, where Virgil had last reposed.

Agatha asked, "You don't see him there, by any chance?"

"See who?" asked Nydia sharply.

"Virgil. You keep sneaking glances at the chair behind the desk as though you expect he might somehow materialize."

"I feel his presence in the room."

"Ah! That bodes well for a successful séance!"

"I'm not too sure."

"Oh? And why's that?"

"I also feel hostility."

"From Virgil? Hostility? He always seemed to me so calm and self-contained. I never witnessed a display of temper."

Bette entered. "Whose display of temper?"

"Virgil's."

"I'm lost. What have I been missing?"

"Nydia feels Virgil's presence and she also feels hostility, possibly his."

"Why should Virgil be hostile? I should think he'd be delighted to hear from us so soon after his departure."

Nydia said with patience, "Wraiths have been known to turn hostile. They cause things to fly about the house. They can raise sudden windstorms of terrifying ferocity. They open doors and then slam them shut. They can turn tap water black and fetid. They can cause disgusting odors to invade one's rooms, and they can cause odd items to disappear."

"Well, if Virgil's going to behave that badly, then I for one am no longer eager to welcome him, whether this is his property or not." She had lit a cigarette and was making her familiar swirling motions with the hand holding it.

"Now, ladies," cautioned Agatha, "let us not foresee the

86

unforeseeable. After all, Virgil may not be all that easy to contact."

"Of course. He may not have reached there yet!" said Bette with good old New England sensibility.

"Reached where?" asked Agatha, possibly suspecting there might be timetables with schedules for arrivals in the afterworld, if such an uncharted territory existed.

Bette shrugged. "Wherever we're trying to reach Virgil. Well, we know for certain he's not in Beverly Hills."

Nydia sat at the head of the table. "His spirit could be en route to Egypt, actually."

Agatha clapped her hands for attention. "We're getting a little silly. I know séances are at times an occasion for giddiness. But I feel we must be very sensible and very serious tonight if we're to impress the police and Virgil's family. Now then, while there's still time before the others arrive: Nydia, you were closest to Virgil. Did he ever discuss his enemies?"

"I don't know if I'd call them enemies. I'm referring to other archeologists who envied and to some extent loathed him."

"To a large extent loathed him. Let's not be coy about the not-all-that-dear departed. I didn't like him at all and he knew it. He admitted he knew it when he visited me last night. On the other hand, my Max liked him very much. Oh, dear!"

"What is it?" asked a concerned Bette.

"Max will be terribly shocked when he hears Virgil's been murdered. I should have thought to cable him before he reads it in the papers. But then, Max doesn't spend time reading newspapers when he's at work." She thought for a moment. "Anyway, Max is a very splendid shock absorber. I'll cable him in the morning. And we heard Roland's side of the story in the basement earlier."

"I would have had it rewritten," commented Bette.

"You didn't believe him?" Agatha's eyebrows were raised.

"Too much about their relationship is contradictory. He

says he and Virgil were partners in one of the ventures, and yet he's strapped for cash, whereas Virgil had enough to pay the national debt, and I assume England has one. Remember, he mentioned a Ptolemy grail Virgil found but Roland never saw. I think he intimated it might be among the treasure he thinks are buried in the grave. Don't you, Agatha?"

"If I were Roland I'd be very very bitter about Virgil, if he had found a way to cut me out of my share. On the other hand, we have to take Roland's word that he and Virgil were partners in that first expedition of Virgil's. Unless somewhere he has a written agreement. And I don't remember him mentioning one."

Bette was at work on a new cigarette. "Let me tell you something I suspect." She took a long drag on the cigarette and then exhaled ferociously, almost asphyxiating Agatha. Bette apologized and revealed her suspicion. "I think that partnership speech is Sir Roland's rather devious way of forming the basis for a claim against Virgil's estate. Stands to reason, doesn't it, ladies?"

"Bette, my dear, I think you've hit on something quite plausible, and I could use an apple."

"Please, Agatha, I can't stand the sound of chomping noises when I'm conducting a séance."

"It'll be on your head if I develop withdrawal symptoms."

Bette resumed. "Let's face it. He stands a better chance of a claim than Anthea and Oscar."

"A very good theory." She rubbed her chin. "Of course, if Virgil has left a lot of that stuff to some place like the British Museum, they'll fight hard against Roland, and they've got the money for a long, hard fight." She scratched her cheek gently. "Anthea and Oscar will probably stand behind Roland with the prospect of being amply rewarded should he win the claim."

Bette asked from out of thin air, "Is there no man in Anthea's life or was there ever?"

"She's had no luck with men. Not while Mabel was alive.

When Anthea brought a young hopeful home for family approval, he was soon enchanted by Mabel, and Anthea became a distant figure on the horizon. No, Anthea was all caught up in her love for Virgil."

"That sounds very unhealthy," commented Bette while picking a piece of tobacco from her tongue.

Nydia said in a small voice, "Are you always given to understatement, Bette?"

"Aha. Seems I've struck oil." Bette waited for more from Nydia.

"I've told this to Agatha, and if she doesn't mind hearing it again, I'll repeat it for you, Bette."

"Please, my dear, go right ahead. Our other guests are late."

Nydia lit a cigarette and then spoke. "I didn't toss Virgil over. I was the one who got the heave-ho. Very gentlemanly, of course, but nevertheless the heave-ho. And as heave-hos go, it was more heave than ho."

"I'm going to love this, I know," said Bette. "All about heave."

"As happens to most of us women trapped in what I for one considered too long a courtship, I finally put it to him squarely: What were his intentions? Well, it turns out his intentions weren't very intense. I had completely misinterpreted him. He was not the marrying kind and all that balderdash, and what he felt towards me were the feelings of an older brother to a younger sister."

"From my experiences with families," said Bette, "that's not very flattering. I hope you slapped his face."

"No, I slapped his ego. I was in a rage, probably very much like those rages Agatha says could lead to murder. I told him that he wasn't man enough to commit himself as a husband and I was bored stiff with him and archeology."

"And yet you continued to bring him vegetable stews." Bette's arms were folded, smoke curling to the ceiling from her cigarette.

Nydia said quickly, "Once I could see he was ill, my maternal instincts took over, and by that time I was no longer interested in him romantically."

"Did you ever sleep with him, for crying out loud?"

"Oh, Bette, you *do* rush in where angels fear to tread," said Agatha.

"No, Bette, I never slept with him. He never made a pass at me or a gentle inquiry. He managed to keep the subject at arm's length."

"Was he a homosexual?"

"I don't know," said Nydia. "He had no special male friend."

"He didn't have to. There are strange places where homosexuals congregate, so I've been told. Public parks, secret bars and tearooms."

"Tearooms?" Agatha was genuinely surprised. "I didn't know America had tearooms."

Bette laughed. "Certain public toilets where homosexuals go *pour le sport.* Those are called tearooms. Polo is the sport of kings, or is it horse racing? And cruising is the sport of queens. Perhaps he was AC/DC."

"Explain again," demanded Agatha, wondering if she could ever use any of this stuff in a future book. To her, homosexuals were like men from Mars. Perhaps they existed or perhaps they didn't. She for one didn't think she'd ever met one.

Bette was explaining, "AC/DC Alternate current or direct current. Alternate for bisexuality, and I've been told there's a lot of that in this country. Something to do with so many private, boys'-only schools. Oh, the hell with it. Are you two hinting there was something unhealthy going on between Anthea and Virgil?"

"One did find oneself wondering at times," said Agatha.

Nydia stated flatly, "I think Virgil was asexual. Mabel drained the blood out of him. As for Anthea, I pity her. I hope Virgil was generous to her. He owes her that."

Bette asked, "What about brother Oscar? If he didn't wear clothes, I think he'd be invisible."

"He does have a terrible temper," said Agatha. "I've witnessed some awful outbursts. Or actually, I overheard some. And I'm sure he's still very bitter at inheriting very little from Mummy. Oh, dear! I did say 'Mummy,' didn't I? Unintentional pun, I promise you. There was a very pointed sibling rivalry among them for Mabel's love and attention. Mabel doted on precociousness and Virgil was very, very precocious. He played Mabel for all she was worth and she adored being played upon. Very stupid and very vain and very beautiful and not worth a *sou* as a mother or a wife."

"Now really, Agatha. Oscar composes music and Anthea writes poetry. Now, in my books *that's* precocious. But my books count for nothing in this story, don't they? Wasn't Sir Roland ever pleased Virgil chose to follow in his footsteps?"

"Until he realized Virgil's feet were larger and were obliterating his footprints. Thanks to Mabel, Virgil was smarter. Sir Roland was an honest man. He turned over a large part of his spoils to museums in the countries he explored. Roland explored. Virgil exploited."

"You just said Mabel was very stupid," stated a bemused Bette.

"I'm sorry. I should have elucidated. I meant stupid about her husband and her children. In financial matters, she was incredibly clever. Having been Roland's investor, she claimed most of what remained and cashed in on it handsomely. Where Roland gave, Mabel traded."

"Why can't I be smart like that?" Bette wondered aloud. "Every dame in Hollywood my age owns a house. Me? I rent! Well, all that's going to change when I win my case." She derailed herself. "Are you sure there wasn't someone special in Virgil's life?"

"Cleopatra," said Nydia.

"Really?" Bette was lighting up again.

"Absolutely. His ambition was to find her tomb."

Agatha shed more light. "That's been every archeologist's ambition for eons upon eons. It lay dormant for a while until a few years ago, when that Colbert person did her Cleopatra for the screen. Rather well too, I thought."

Bette interrupted, "I would have played the death scene *much* differently. Claudette used the tiniest of asps." She exhaled. "I'd have pressed a cobra to my bosom." She looked at the ceiling and asked, "Claudette, where is thy sting?" Then she changed tack again. "Why wasn't Virgil ever caught? Stealing all those artifacts. Filling his basement with contraband. How'd he get them out of Egypt? How'd he get them into England?"

"The fiddle, my dear Bette, the fiddle," said Agatha.

"Another British expression that demands explaining."

"Bribes, my dear, bribes. Virgil had a wonderful nose for smelling out which officials had Achilles heels. And we are living in very hard times. Of course, times aren't hard for Nydia and myself and others like us, because in my case I earn and in Nydia's case she inherited. But minor officials earn very little money and are susceptible to temptation. And, my dear, as your wonderful Mae West has said, 'There's nothing so tempting as temptation.'"

Bette looked around the room and at its magnificent treasures as they heard the door chimes. "To think the family once lived together under this roof."

Agatha said, "They couldn't stomach living here after Mabel's will left them more or less financially stranded. With what money they had, they found modest lodgings of their own, and as far as I know, those are the lodgings they now inhabit. Of course, Anthea continued haunting this place, and if luck is on our side, Virgil's taken over."

"Only temporarily, I hope," cried Bette.

Agatha said, "They're beginning to arrive at last."

"Let's greet them in the drawing room," suggested Bette, and without waiting for any demurrals she led the way out of the library. Agatha followed on her heels while Nydia remained behind for a moment, staring at the chair behind the desk.

The arrivals were Inspector Cayman and Detective Nayland, Mamby having already installed them in the drawing room. Mamby told Bette she'd be bringing in the coffee immediately while Bette asked the men if they preferred something stronger. Coffee was the unanimous choice, and Mamby hurried to bring it. Nydia joined them, and Agatha asked if she had lingered in the library to check on the hostility she thought she had sensed earlier. Agatha told Cayman and Nayland about Nydia's presentiment and explained that she and Nydia and Bette had given the Wynns and their past a fairly thorough going-over.

"I hope you'll share all of that with me," said Cayman. He looked at his wristwatch. "I thought the Wynns would be here by now. It's past eight."

"Punctuality was never their strong suit," explained Agatha, "a quality inherited from Mabel where the children are concerned, a chronic disability on Sir Roland's part. I'll sketch this in quickly." She had the police officers' undivided attention while she recapped what had been discussed in the library, stopping every so often to ask Bette and Nydia if she was getting it right. She was, and she knew she was, but she thought it politic to defer to one or the other every so often.

When Agatha had concluded, Cayman said, "Thank you. There's lots of food there for thought." He added slyly, "Along with that fed Virgil Wynn to hasten his path to the boneyard."

"God!" exclaimed Bette.

"I do get a bit colorful every now and then, Bette. It helps to keep me from going round the bend. One has to be truly devoted to be a detective, and I am truly devoted, which means I'm in for long, tedious, and tiresome periods digging up facts; investigating leads, mostly false; battling officialdom; and taking too many aspirin." Nellie Mamby arrived with the tea cart, now carrying coffee, china, silverware, a bowl of sugar, and a pitcher of milk. "Ah! Florence Nightingale!" Mamby shot him a look of disapproval.

"Have you the results of the autopsy?" Agatha asked Cayman as Bette mimed to Mamby that she should serve the coffee, which Mamby set to do with her usual proficiency.

"I do, and Ambrose MacDougal asked me to remember him to you."

Agatha asked, "Who is Ambrose MacDougal?"

"How fleeting is fame," said Cayman. "Ambrose is the coroner. It was he who carted Virgil off to the morgue."

"Ambrose MacDougal. You must forgive me. I have a terrible time with names, especially those of the small-part players."

"I'll remember not to tell him that, because he admires you tremendously. You were absolutely right about the poison and the symptoms and the effect, but there was something you missed."

"And what was that?" asked Agatha, her voice rising a pitch.

"There was a stab wound to the back of his neck, from a weapon plunged into his mouth. It severed an artery. Had you opened his mouth to examine his teeth, you would have found a very ugly scene."

Bette said shrilly, "Well, I for one am glad Agatha kept his mouth shut!"

Nydia said, "So he was meeting someone here. That's the real reason he rushed away from the dinner."

They heard Mamby gasp, "Oh, my God. He was murdered here while I slept?"

Cayman asked, "Are you sure it was when you were asleep?"

"I didn't hear any carryings-on last night. I go to bed early unless there's something special on the wireless. And I've told you my room is in the back of the house. I didn't hear anything." She paused to think. "I did have the wireless on! Gracie Fields was doing a concert. And when she sings, you can't hear anything else, don't you agree?"

"I'd love to," said Cayman, "but I'm not a fan of Gracie

Fields and I turn on the wireless only to hear the news read. And there's the front door. The Wynns have arrived."

Grateful for the reprieve, Nellie Mamby hurried to the front door.

Bette said to Cayman, "You've frightened her."

Cayman said smoothly, "Your Nellie Mamby probably knows more of what has gone on in this house than any previous inhabitant. She's the only person in service?"

"The one and only," said Bette. "At least she's all I've inherited."

Agatha told them, "When Mabel did her salons, she hired extra help. And if I recall correctly, there's a woman who comes in weekly to help with the cleaning. It's a large house, but not all of it is used, not since Virgil was left to live on his own."

"Poor Virgil," moaned Nydia.

"Rich Virgil," corrected Agatha.

"A lot of good his wealth does him now," said Nydia.

"Our apologies," said Sir Roland, "but we treated ourselves to the beef at Simpson's on the Strand, forgetting we'd be caught up in the theater traffic." He said to Bette, "So many theaters on the Strand, my dear. It's as bad as Shaftesbury Avenue."

"Worse," said Oscar. "I see there's coffee. We didn't have time for coffee. I wonder, Bette, could we prevail on you to ask Nellie to prepare a fresh pot?"

Nellie spoke up swiftly. "There's plenty fresh in the urn. I only just served it. Can't you see it's one of the big ones we used to use for the parties?"

Bette said with exaggerated patience, "Mamby, please serve the others." She added something in a new tone of voice that told Agatha that, under the actress's professional facade, there lay a vixen ready to pounce if provoked. Agatha found Bette fascinating, and she suspected Cayman was also intrigued. The new tone of voice said, "Inspector Cayman has some fascinating news for you, don't you, Inspector?"

Anthea asked, "You mean Virgil wasn't poisoned after all? It was some form of disease that killed him?"

"Oh, your brother was most certainly being poisoned in small doses that were about to take deadly effect. I also believe some form of disease also killed him. The disease known as greed." He heard Oscar's quick intake of breath. Sir Roland glared at his son, while Anthea's face remained unreadable. Inspector Cayman shocked the Wynns with the facts about Virgil's fatal stab wound in the mouth.

"How terrible," said Oscar, his voice small and listless.

"I'm a bit confused," said Sir Roland. "How could such a wound be inflicted?" Surely Virgil would have been loath to have his mouth pried open."

"I'm sure such a step was unnecessary. Nayland, be a good chap and sit in the chair behind the desk. Now then, let us assume that Virgil was having an argument with Mr. or Miss X. His adversary says something that makes Virgil throw his head back with laughter . . ."

Nydia exclaimed, "That's quite true! He was one of those hearty laughers! He used to be terribly embarrassing in the theater. He always threw his head back and bellowed."

"Just like his mother," said Sir Roland wistfully.

"Nayland, be a good chap and throw your head back with your mouth wide open. No need for sound effects." Nayland was grateful for that. "Now, in a fit of anger, the killer plunges the weapon into Virgil's mouth, and *voilá*, Virgil is dispatched with dispatch."

Bette, hands on hips, asked, "Where'd he get the weapon? Did he bring it with him?"

"There was a weapon on the desk," said Agatha. "Don't any of you recall? You certainly should, Roland. You said it came from Baramar's tomb. You used it as a letter opener. And later, so did Virgil."

"Ah, yes, of course! The Baramar dagger. But where is it now?" Sir Roland was looking around him as though he expected to find the weapon on the floor near the desk.

"It's certainly not here," said Cayman. He asked Bette and Nydia, "Was there any sign of it when you found the body?"

"If there had been," said Bette, "I'm sure we'd have brought it to your attention."

"It's quite valuable," said Sir Roland.

"Then I might have hocked it," said Bette dryly.

"Hocked it?" questioned Cayman.

"Pawned it," explained Bette.

Cayman expounded quite seriously, "You'd have a difficult time pawning a relic, I should think."

"I should think you would think," said Bette with a smile. "Oh, come on, Inspector. I'm just kidding."

"Yes. Of course. Kidding. American jocularity. Now then," he said seriously, "there's to be an inquest scheduled, of course. To avoid too much notoriety, I suggest we schedule times for you to appear at Scotland Yard tomorrow for questioning. I wish to see Sir Roland, Oscar, and Anthea Wynn, Nellie Mamby, and, of course, you, Miss Tilson."

Nydia's eyes narrowed. "What do you mean by 'of course' me?"

"Vegetable stew, to begin with. And I'm not interested in the recipe. And you did have an intimate relationship with Virgil Wynn."

"I can assure you it was no reason to lead to murder."

Yes it could have, thought Bette as she lit a cigarette. You said so yourself to Agatha and me. You got so mad when he said he had no intention of marrying you, you might very well have killed him on the spot. Agatha caught her eye. Very subtly she put an index finger to her lips. Bette responded with a wink, assuring the author she was pledged to silence.

Cayman assigned Nayland to set up appointments for tomorrow with the five suspects, after which the séance could commence. Nellie Mamby fretted, while Cayman was good enough to calm and reassure her. Bette heard him say this would be quite painless, not like a trip to the dentist. Agatha took the opportunity to draw Bette to the urn, where she refilled her cup. She whispered, "Let Nydia handle this in her own fashion. She's quite capable of looking after herself."

"Do you think she might have killed him?"

"For what reason? I won't say rejection is too slim a motive, because that depends on the disposition of the person suspected. I've known Nydia much too long. She's a good friend and she was a good wife. At least I never heard her husband complain."

"Where'd his money come from?"

"Inherited. Very old money."

"I dream of very new money," said Bette. "And yet, Agatha, there's the vegetable stew."

"Very old recipe. Handed down for generations. Very good too. Takes careful preparation. I've tried it. No use. I suppose you have to have a special talent for it. Ah, Inspector! You certainly enjoyed your bombshell!"

"Am I interrupting something private?" he asked genially.

"You would have, a minute earlier," said Bette.

"Tell me, Inspector," began Agatha as she stirred sugar into her coffee. "How come I'm not to be interrogated?" He didn't reply immediately, so she took up the slack with a further dissertation. "After all, I loathed the man. He was a nasty blot on the worthy profession of my husband, and in general I found him mean and incredibly boring."

"Despite the fact that your husband found something likable about him?"

"Max finds something likable about everything. We must arrange for you to meet my husband. He's really quite charming, and he loves to swap dirty jokes, as I'm sure you do. Well, you do, don't you? You're a policeman." She said to Bette, "They swap jokes to relieve the monotony. Detective work, like archeology, is a hard slog. And it's even harder when you fictionalize it, as I can well tell you. Another thing, Inspector. I have no alibi. I was home alone, but I have no proof."

"Why are you so anxious to be considered a suspect?"

"Why, my dear, sweet man, to throw you off the scent. Why else?"

"You mean to throw me off someone else's scent. Probably your friend Miss Tilson."

"Young man, you're too clever."

7

Nayland interrupted them to show Cayman the schedule for the next day's questioning. "I set them two hours apart, beginning at nine in the morning with Nellie Mamby. She's the earliest riser. Miss Tilson asked to be scheduled the last, as, she explained, séances take a great deal out of her and so she sleeps late the next morning."

"She sleeps late, séance or no séance," said Agatha. Cayman took Nayland by the arm and led him away.

Bette asked Agatha, "Do you really want to be cross-examined?"

"Of course not. It's all so boring and tedious. What I really want to do is cross-examine the inspector. There's so much fodder here for a new book! A real murder beats dreaming one up."

"Agatha, you didn't by any chance notice the dagger this morning?"

"I didn't, dear, because it wasn't in the room. The murderer disposed of it."

"You mean he . . ."

". . . or she . . ."

". . . took it with him . . ."

". . . or her . . ."

"So it's gone."

"I don't think so."

"You mean it's here, somewhere in the house?"

"Absolutely. What better place to hide it? Think, my dear, think. As my Hercule Poirot would say, 'Use your little gray cells.' If a midget wanted to hide, where best to hide but in a room full of midgets?" She smiled. "And if you wanted to hide an artifact in this house . . ."

"The basement!"

"Not so loud. We don't want to give the game away."

"I'm sure it's occurred to the inspector."

"Of course. He's quite good. A bit too flirtatious for my taste, but still a very good sleuth."

"You think he's flirting with you?"

"Don't be so dense. He's flirting with you, and you like it."

"You've noticed. And I've been trying so hard to be subtle about it. I feel so guilty."

"Why? You've sent your husband packing. You're a free soul. Flirt away, and to hell with the rest."

"But he left only a few days ago. One of those awful boats that carry cargo."

"All boats carry cargo dear, and he's probably carrying on a flagrant flirtation of his own with a wealthy divorcée he met in the ship's saloon."

"You think so?"

"He's on the rebound. He's a man. He's lonely, and the sea air has whetted his appetite."

"The beast. I hope she treats him like dirt."

Nydia had opened one of the doors of the French window that led to the garden and she drank heavily of the night air. "We're in luck," she announced to no one in particular. "The air is fresh and crisp. The night is clear. The moon is full."

Bette wondered if she was going to break into song. Each line she spoke would have made an appropriate cue for a ballad.

"A full moon. This augurs well for a good séance."

"A full moon?" Bette sounded anxious as she twirled her right hand. "Doesn't that often signify trouble? Werewolves?"

"Don't forget witches on broomsticks and screeching black cats with their backs up," reminded Agatha. "This is not All Hallows' Eve, Bette, Halloween to you, this is just an ordinary night, and be grateful there's no fog. A fog could cloud Nydia's communications."

Nydia turned to them, arms outflung, like an operatic diva responding to cries for an encore. "Shall we commence?" She shepherded them to the library, walking briskly, as though having frequently rehearsed the possibility of being the mistress of the house.

Sir Roland, walking with Cayman, asked, "Does Scotland Yard frequently countenance a séance?"

"I can't recall that it has. At any rate, this one is an extracurricular thing on my part. I've attended several before. Some very good, some absolute nonsense. I'm anxious to see how Miss Tilson conducts one. She has such a remarkably good reputation."

"Nydia is remarkable in many ways," said Sir Roland somewhat mysteriously.

Agatha had an arm around Anthea's shoulders. "You're so quiet, my dear. I miss the chatter."

"I'm frightened."

"Yes?" Agatha was eager for more.

"That's all I can tell you. I'm frightened. I don't like this house anymore. There's evil here."

"Dare I ask, has your father made any arrangements as to Virgil's interment?"

"That's what we discussed at dinner. There's the family vault. You know it. That's where Mother reposes."

And soon, thought Agatha, she'll be co-reposing with her favorite child. She wondered if in the afterlife Mabel was holding her salons. There'd be so many celebrities to capture! Imagine a salon in which Marie Antoinette was discussing hairdressers with Mary, Queen of Scots. Indeed, a very heady subject, thought Agatha, and then she reminded herself she disliked both historical ladies.

Bette surveyed the table and asked, "Does it matter where we sit?"

"Sit wherever you like and be comfortable." Sir Roland saw to it that he sat next to Bette. Inspector Cayman was on her left. Agatha sat on his left. Bette hoped this was one of those séances where you had to touch fingers with the person seated on either side of you. She wanted very much to touch Cayman's fingers. She wasn't so sure about Sir Roland, but at least she'd know she'd be safe from any sudden pincers movement on his part. Nydia was at the head of the table. On her right was Anthea, and Oscar was seated on her left. Nayland sat between Anthea and Nellie Mamby and was positive Mamby's fingers would be icy cold. Mamby had drawn the drapes as instructed before taking her seat. The table's center-piece was a unique candelabra that held two candles.

Nydia said in a tone of voice that Bette feared might lead to some mystic incantation, "Now, let me caution you. Sometimes nothing happens for quite a while. We mustn't become impatient or discouraged. The spirits move at a pace all their own."

Not all that spirited, then, thought Bette. She asked, "Can the spirits be dangerous?"

Nydia explained, "They are sometimes mischievous. They do have their impish moments, but not too often. Mostly, I find the spirits very receptive, as anxious to hear from us as we are anxious to contact them."

"I see," said Bette gaily. "Like actors waiting to hear from their agents." Agatha shot her a cautionary look. "Nydia, have you someone special who links you with the afterlife?"

"I have several, dear. One must have more than one, as there are so many séances being conducted all over the world at the same time that they tend to crowd each other. In fact I was invited to another séance tonight in Hampstead, but the man conducting it has a difficult stammer, so it takes him twice as long to contact his go-between."

Bette asked again, "How will we know if there's a spirit present?"

"Usually they rap."

"What if they don't give a rap?"

"Please, Bette, no frivolity." She inhaled deeply. "Oh! Oh! Oh! I feel the powers gathering. They're beginning to course through my veins. That's a very good sign, a very very good sign."

So she has good circulation, thought Bette, and then caught herself before vocalizing the observation.

Nydia said breathless, "Mamby . . . light the candles . . . then put out the other lights."

Bette said, "What an unusual candelabrum. I meant to ask its origin when I noticed it this morning. You know, after the shock of . . . well, you know . . ."

"We know," rasped Agatha.

Sir Roland whispered to her, "About five hundred years B.C. It's one of my discoveries."

The candlelight glistened. The room was in semidarkness. Mamby returned to her seat. She ran her thin tongue around her dry, even thinner lips. She longed for a shot of gin.

Nydia said, "Now, everyone, spread your fingers so that your pinkies touch."

Bette said sternly under her breath to Sir Roland, "We're supposed to be touching pinkies, and *that's all.*"

Though there wasn't the slightest hint of a breeze in the room, the candles were flickering. Bette reveled in Cayman's slight touch. Cayman looked into Bette's eyes and saw the candlelight reflected. Bette felt a *frisson* and knew she was blushing. Nydia was intoning what Bette assumed was some mystic chant used by spiritualists to stir up activity in the afterworld. It wasn't Nydia's voice, or at least not the voice with which Bette was familiar. Agatha's eyes were closed and

Bette wondered if she was dozing. She hoped Cayman wasn't feeling rejected because she had moved her eyes away from his. Constant staring at an object made her eyes cross and she didn't want the inspector to think she had imperfections. Her nervous habit of twirling her hands when she was agitated was bad enough, and the way she clipped each word when she spoke was considered an affectation. Although her mannerisms were odd, they were fascinating and uniquely her own. She was not yet aware that she was an unique original, such as Garbo and Crawford. In this room and at this moment she was feeling neither unique nor original. She was wondering what the hell she was doing participating in something that was looked upon as an amusing aberration where she came from. The thought of anyone conducting a séance in Lowell, Massachusets, almost made her giggle.

Cayman whispered to her, "You're fidgeting. Are you uncomfortable?"

Bette whispered back, "I wish Nydia would switch stations. Nothing's happening. Maybe the spirits are out to dinner."

"Nydia warned us it might be this way for a while."

Nydia, thought Bette, not Miss Tilson. Has he been flirting with Nydia too? If he has, she hasn't noticed. But then, he's terribly subtle. Is there a Mrs. Cayman? she wondered. And if so, are there little Caymans crawling about underfoot?

Nydia gasped. She didn't resume chanting. Her face was aglow. Even in the dim light Bette recognized the transformation. *"Bon soir, ma chère. Ça va?"*

"Oh, brother," said Bette. "Isn't that French she's speaking?"

"Excellent accent," said Cayman.

"Maybe it isn't her. Doesn't sound like her. I wish she had subtitles. I don't understand French." Bette was getting annoyed, when Nydia suddenly switched to English.

Agatha said, "She's talking to Joan of Arc."

"Are you sure?" asked Sir Roland.

"This isn't the first time she's gotten through to her. Jeanne d'Arc's terribly garrulous. The last time there was no shutting her up. She's very overwrought when all fired up."

Nydia interrupted, "This is not Joan. This is an actress who says she was once under contract to MGM. She wants to speak to Bette. She's dying for some news of Hollywood. She's sipping an *apéritif* with John Gilbert. Her name is Renée Adorée."

"Oh, of course," cried Bette. "She died three years ago. TB. She did several silents with Mr. Gilbert."

Now Nydia was speaking with a French accent. "Hello, Bette Davis. I am Renée Adorée. We have never met."

"No, no we haven't," said Bette nervously. "How's John Gilbert taking heaven?"

"By storm."

"You *are* speaking from heaven, aren't you?" Bette felt like a fool. She was positive Nydia was making this all up. And yet, she was carrying it off magnificently. Except for Cayman, who had a very pronounced look of cynicism, the others were transfixed.

"John wants to ask: Do you know if Marlene Dietrich still mourns him? She has such a short attention span."

"To paraphrase the words of the late Priscilla Mullens, 'Why doesn't John speak for himself?' "

"He has laryngitis."

"Oh, dear. I am truly sorry. Give him lots of hot tea laced with rum and sweet butter. It's my mother's recipe, and it always has worked for me. As to Marlene, I'm afraid I don't know her and I can't tell him if she's still in mourning. But if I were he, I'd go hunting in greener pastures. There's bound to be some available tootsie or other on Cloud Nine."

"Bette!" snapped Agatha. Cayman smothered a laugh in a fit of coughing. Nayland was staring at Nellie Mamby on his left. She was breathing heavily, abnormally. He wondered if she was suffering from a respiratory ailment. Agatha was also staring at Mamby. She leaned over and asked, "Are you all right?"

"I'm frightened."

"There's nothing to be frightened of."

"I think there is."

"You're wrong. Just relax and listen to Mrs. Tilson."

"I think she's daft." But Nellie Mamby started to relax.

Nydia said, her voice now lyrical, "*Como está usted, Conchita?*"

Agatha smiled. "Ah, yes! La Conchita! We haven't had her in a long time. She was a famous flamenco dancer." She asked Nydia, "Where's she been all this time?"

"On tour," replied Nydia.

Agatha explained to the others, "Perhaps you may remember La Conchita. She was struck down by a lorry in Covent Garden, on her way to the Royal Opera to dance in *Carmen*. The lorry crushed her but not her castanets."

"Oh, my God! My ears!" cried Nydia. "Stop clacking those God-damned things in my ears." Nydia was berating La Conchita in Castilian Spanish.

Bette said, "I'm terribly impressed. Nydia speaks so many languages. I wonder," she asked slyly. "Does she talk Turkey?" Agatha shot her a look that warned Bette to hold her tongue.

Agatha said, "You have to talk in many languages in this business. Often, Nydia isn't aware she's speaking a foreign tongue. You see, it is not really Nydia speaking. It is the deceased, using her as a medium of communication. That's why spiritualists are known as mediums."

Nydia interrupted, "At last! Yes! It's you, isn't it, Virgil? Yes, yes, it's me. It's your iron maiden."

Agatha said to the others, "Virgil called her that because she can at times be very boorishly stubborn."

Bette was interested. "Do you think he'll tell us who stabbed him?"

It was uncanny, but it seemed as though Virgil's voice were emanating from Nydia's mouth. "There's safety in numbers."

Agatha scolded, "Virgil, we haven't spent this time contacting you to hear clichés. Who stabbed you?"

"Oh, stop scolding him, Agatha," screeched Nydia.

"Oh, my God, it's Mabel!" shouted Sir Roland.

"Mother? Is that you? It's me. It's Oscar!"

"Oh, do shut up, Oscar! You're always interrupting! Why can't you be more like your brother?"

"I hate my brother! I've always hated my brother! You were both against me!"

Anthea suddenly chimed in shrilly, "They were always against us!"

"Hush, children, hush," cautioned Sir Roland. "Remember your mother's blood pressure."

"Oh, bugger her blood pressure," shouted Anthea. Her voice took on a nasty edge. "It's nice to hear from you, Mother." She ground down on the word 'Mother.' "Tell us, *Mother*, why did you take an overdose? *Mother!*" Silence. "Damn you, Nydia. Don't lose her!"

Bette said to Cayman lustily, "Now, *this* is worth the price of admission."

"Quiet. I don't want to miss any of this," he said harshly.

There was one spirit in the room that was beginning to sink, and it was Bette's. She suspected Cayman was beginning to lose interest in her.

Nydia had resumed speaking as Mabel. Her voice was soft, modulated. "It wasn't at all bitter. It was so easy to drink. I wasn't at all afraid. I was so sure I'd be afraid of Death. I'd seen that film *Death Takes a Holiday*, with that sexy Fredric March playing Death, and I remember thinking, If that's what Death looks like, then make way for Mabel, with a tallyho and a yoicks yoicks yoicks."

"You are so vulgar, Mabel!" shouted Sir Roland.

Mabel snapped back, "You didn't marry me for my manners and my kindly disposition. You married me for my money, and I married you because at the time there was little else about. I married you because I was desperate to lose my virginity!"

Sir Roland was roaring with laughter. "You've lost your virginity so often you belong in a book of records! You slut!"

Nydia as Mabel said in a singsong, "I'm certainly glad I left you very little in my will. And that goes for you too, Oscar, you po-faced nincompoop. And as for you Anthea . . ."

Anthea's hands flew up and covered her ears. "I don't want to hear it! I don't want to hear it! Go away, you terrible woman!"

Nydia said as Mabel, "Would you prefer I recited some of your priceless blank verse?"

Slowly, Anthea lowered her hands. She was unusually calm and self-contained. "That would be terribly interesting, Mother, considering I never recited any for you or asked you to read it."

Nydia as Mabel laughed eerily, and Bette had the feeling she was asleep in a horrible nightmare from which she was having a terrible time trying to awaken. She looked at Agatha, whose expression told her nothing. It told Cayman a great deal. Mrs. Mallowan was listening and absorbing and interpreting and learning a great deal from these colloquies with the supposed unknown. Bette's eyes moved from Agatha to Nydia and then on to Cayman, and all of a sudden she began to feel very, very wise.

Virgil was back. "There's safety in numbers."

"Oh, not that again," whispered Bette.

It was repeated. "There's safety in numbers."

Agatha spoke up. "What do you mean by that, Virgil? Is that a clue? Is that a key to the identity of your murderer? What is 'There's safety in numbers' supposed to tell us?"

Bette spoke up swiftly. "I think he means that because we're all seated around the table touching pinkies, except for Anthea, who's broken the link, there's no chance of the murderer striking again, not here, not during the séance."

Sir Roland asked, "You think someone else is going to be murdered?"

"Sir Roland," said Bette, "I'm not quite sure if someone is or isn't. But I have some very powerful instincts. I live a great deal by my instincts. And something tells me that, like some insatiably oversexed rabbit, the murderer is breeding another victim."

The people in this room she cared about the most, Agatha and the inspector, were looking at her with admiration. Detective Nayland thought her a fool. The murderer could interpret what she had just said as a threat to his or her identity. Nayland was also wondering why Cayman was looking like an Oxford don pleased with a very smart student. His eyes darted from face to face. Sir Roland looked drained. Oscar's eyes were blinking nervously. Anthea's eyes were misted with tears. Nellie Mamby looked on the verge of fainting. Agatha and Cayman were exchanging smiles. Obviously they and Bette Davis had heard something he hadn't heard, which probably explained why they had made some headway in their professional fields.

Nydia shouted in her own voice, "Virgil! Don't go yet! You haven't explained yourself! What do you mean by 'There's safety in numbers'?"

"Perhaps he's suggesting a flutter at a betting parlor," said Agatha, fanning herself with a hand. It had grown terribly close in the library.

"Virgil! You can't leave us hanging like this!"

Unfortunate choice of words, thought Cayman, as someone in this room will certainly hang for the crime of murder.

Agatha said, "Oh, do release, Virgil. He must have had an exhausting journey."

Nydia's moan was followed by a sharp intake of breath. Then, with a sigh, her head fell forward.

Agatha commanded, "Mamby, the lights."

Bette was worried about Nydia. "Is she all right?"

"Yes, yes, of course she is," reassured Agatha. "She expends so much energy, it leaves her drained until her first glass of Scotch whisky."

The room was flooded with light. Agatha wetted the tips of a thumb and an index finger and extinguished the candles. Slowly, Nydia's eyes opened. With an effort she sat up.

Bette spoke to Mamby. "Mamby, I think drinks would be very welcome. Shall we return to the drawing room?" It suddenly occurred to Bette to ask Agatha, "Why are they called 'drawing rooms'? Nobody draws in them, as far as I know." They were leaving the library, arm in arm.

"As far as anybody knows, my dear, and stop trying to pull the wool over my eyes."

"Meaning?"

"Meaning whether you think Nydia's performance was that of a very good fraud or a very good actress, there was a lot of what she spoke that I suspect you interpreted as suggestive of being clues."

"Nydia, I gather, knows a hell of a lot about the Wynn family and the Wynn murders, and something tells me she's gone a little too far. She could be in danger."

"She could be. So could you. You're alone in this house from tonight onward." She smiled slyly. "You might need protection. Perhaps you should invite the inspector to spend the night."

"Why, Mrs. Mallowan, for shame. The idea of thinking I'm one of those kinds of women who hop into bed at the drop of a pair of trousers."

"Actually, I don't. But something you just said is puzzling me."

"I say a lot of things that puzzle people. I never know why, but it seems I do. What did I say? What was it?"

"It was something you said about Nydia. That she seems to know a great deal about the Wynn family and the Wynn *murders*."

"I don't deny that."

"But I only know that Virgil Wynn was murdered. Do you suspect Mabel was also murdered?"

"As a matter of fact, I do. '*It wasn't at all bitter. It was so easy to drink. I wasn't at all afraid.*' Am I fairly accurate? I learn lines very quickly."

"I should say, Bette, you quoted Mabel verbatim."

"You should say, Agatha, I quoted *Nydia* verbatim." She smiled, and Agatha considered patting her on the head.

"WHAT ARE YOU TWO CONSPIRING ABOUT?" asked Cayman holding a glass of what looked to Bette like gin.

"We're talking about murder," said Bette gaily, "Agatha's favorite subject."

"And mine," added Cayman. Nellie Mamby arrived with two Scotch whiskies on a tray.

"I knew you'd want these," said Mamby.

"Feeling better?" asked Cayman.

"Better?" she inquired innocently.

"Mr. Nayland said you took a turn at the table during the séance."

"It was shortness of breath. I always get short of breath when I get nervous."

"What was there to be nervous about?"

"The spooks!"

Bette wondered when Mamby had appointed herself the comedy relief. She wasn't very funny, in fact not funny at all, and Bette admitted to herself that she didn't much like the woman. But she was stuck with her and she knew she'd have to make the best of a bad situation.

Cayman continued, "You mean you were frightened by the possibility of spirits attending the séance?"

Mamby said ferociously, "Well, you heard what came out of her mouth, didn't you? She's done her mumbo jumbo before in this house. Only those times she was after Egyptian princes and princesses and she spoke hieroglyphics." Bette was amazed she knew the word, let alone could pronounce it.

Cayman asked, "You sat in on those séances too?"

"Mr. Wynn insisted. He didn't want me wandering about the house. He said it would disturb the spirits."

Or disturb the treasures in the basement, thought Bette. She wished Cayman would send the woman away. She wished Cayman and Agatha and herself could quietly examine and dissect Nydia's performance. And it was certainly a performance and a very good one at that. She was a terrific mimic. Certainly her Virgil was right on the nose, though her Renée Adorée could have been any woman with a French accent, such as Fifi D'Orsay, except that Fifi was still among the living. Who at the table could truly recognize Renée's voice? She had been dead at least three years now, and her few talkies had been made at a time when recording voices for film was primitive, and in the case of many silent-screen stars, it sounded their death knell in movies. Bette couldn't attest to the accuracy of Mabel Wynn's voice. She sounded to Bette like a cross between the two top Hollywood character actresses, Mary Boland and Billie Burke.

Deep in thought, Bette had wandered away from the others. The three Wynns and Nydia were huddled around the coffee table and having a spirited exchange, the Wynns being spirited and Nydia wishing she could make an exchange.

Nydia.

Bette realized now she knew very little about her. She made great claims to great wealth. She lived as though she had great wealth. Bette had been vastly impressed by her two-story flat in Cadogan Square. Much too much space for a woman alone, thought Bette when she was there, but she said nothing to Nydia.

Nydia.

A respected spiritualist. Considered one of the best practicing. Based, Bette decided, on her expertise as an actress. To be a good medium, one must try to find out as much as possible about one's clients and their friends. She undoubtedly has given private sessions. She must have access to a great deal of information. And then it struck Bette. Nydia must confine her clients to those with celebrity. It's easy to learn a lot about them. Newspapers. Magazine. Gossip columns. Odd bits of information gleaned here and there, at dinner parties, cocktail parties, weddings, funerals, and bar mitzvahs.

Nydia.

She knows a great deal about me now. I unburdened myself to her on the boat and I haven't stopped unburdening myself ever since. Oh, Christ! Supposing I'm murdered. Supposing she holds a séance. Why, damn it, I'm a cinch for impersonators. The cigarette in the twirling hand, the oversized eyes, the distinct way I walk. Ever since *Of Human Bondage* I've been impersonated by everyone in nightclubs. Well, at least, almost everyone. She'd once been to Finocchio's in San Francisco, the most notorious homosexual nightclub in the United States, and saw twelve men in drag all do impersonations of her at once. It was an incredibly eerie performance, like having twelve out-of-body experiences. She recalled Mae West once telling her that she loved to watch her many impersonators because she learned so much about herself from them.

Bette had learned so much from Nydia. The séance was an epiphany. She was positive Agatha and Cayman, in addition to herself, now suspected Mabel Wynn had been murdered. But by whom?

"*There's safety in numbers.*"

"Now, what the hell's that all about?"

Agatha was at her side. "You're talking to yourself, dear."

"I've got a lot to talk about."

"And we shall talk together, much later, my dear. You, the

inspector, and myself. Now, come join the others. There's small talk, but small talk can often be very revelatory." She took Bette's hand and led her to the others.

Bette sat on the sofa next to Nydia. "I'm very impressed, Nydia. I had no idea spiritualists expended so much energy. When did you realize you had the talent for this sort of thing?"

"It began almost ten years ago. My husband was invited to a séance given by some Indian friends of his. He took me along because I expressed great curiosity. One of the Indians was a professional magician and he wanted to contact Harry Houdini to see if he could get the master to share some of his professional secrets with him."

"Never Houdini," said Agatha grandly. "I knew him when he was doing an extended engagement here the year before his unfortunate death. I wanted to base a character on him, and in order to do so accurately, I arranged to meet him and ask him to divulge some of his secrets. I wasn't the least bit interested in how he sawed a woman in half, because it was obvious there was a false panel in the bottom of the box to accommodate her torso while he sawed away. Mr. Houdini was most charming, as was his very possessive wife. Mr. Houdini charmed away for the better part of half an hour, at the end of which I had learned nothing but her recipe for Russian beet soup. His secrets are buried with him."

"Well, Rama Singh—that was his name, if I recall correctly—was determined to contact Houdini. There were six of us at the séance and it went much the same as it went tonight. Abada Shapoor was the medium. He has since died. Shapoor was highly respected. His reputation was made when at a séance in Buckingham Palace." She explained in an aside, "One of Queen Mary's secret passions is the study of the occult. At any rate, he was conducting this séance and raised Queen Victoria scolding Prince Albert, with Benjamin Disraeli remonstrating on poor Albert's behalf. Let me tell you, I was terribly skeptical from the moment we sat in a circle round the table. There was incense burning, and it was a very heady and somewhat sickening odor. In addition to Abada, Rama, my husband, and myself, there was a *London Times* reporter named Morton Digby and a lady friend of his whose name I can't remember. In attendance were two male servants who saw to the lights or whatever else might be required. Well, as one of the attendants lit the candles in the candelabrum in the center of the table, Abada suddenly said, 'There is a disturbance in this room,' or something like that. I thought perhaps my skepticism was being a bit overpowering, but it was something else. He felt the presence of a power as great as his, if not greater, which was something I'm sure he found difficult to admit, as he turned out to have a monstrous ego. Rama Singh pursuaded him continue regardless of this disturbance, real or imagined, and we touched fingers, and I'm not sure what happened, but it seemed I suddenly dozed off. What soon transpired I'm telling you secondhand, because my husband told me all this later, when we got home."

Listening to Nydia's narrative and looking at the others in the room, Bette was put in mind of the Mad Hatter's tea party. She had expected Nydia to shrug off her question or answer in a few short, succinct sentences. This was more than Bette cared to learn. But when she saw that Agatha and Cayman were giving Nydia their undivided attention, she thought it wise to follow suit. Oscar was picking imaginary lint from his trousers while Sir Roland stifled a yawn and Anthea looked as though she had slipped into a coma.

"It seemed I was talking in a very thick Dutch accent."

"Was it a woman speaking?" asked Cayman.

"It was indeed. She was saying, 'I do not want the handkerchief around my eyes. I want to see my assassins as they pull the triggers.' Well, it was Mata Hari!"

"The spy person?" asked Sir Roland. "Wasn't she a bit of a whore?"

Nydia ignored his question and went on, "And then, and I really thought Ogden was pulling my leg . . .'"

So that was his name, thought Bette. She'd never heard Nydia speak his name before.

"He said I sang part of an aria from *The Bohemian Girl.* You know opera so well, Agatha, you must recognize the song 'I Dreamt I Dwelt in Radclyffe Hall.' "

"It's 'I Dreamt I Dwelt in Marble Halls,' dear."

"Yes, of course. That's what I meant. Well, it was Jenny Lind singing!" She sipped her drink. "And my dears, I can't sing a note. I'm completely atonal. Even when I try to hum it sounds like gargling."

"How did your husband die?" All eyes were on Bette.

"Ogden?"

"That's your husband's name."

"What an odd question. What makes you ask?"

"I'm just curious. This is the first you've ever mentioned his name."

"I've never spoken his name before?"

"Not to me you haven't."

"My poor darling suffered a heart attack. It was quite sudden. At dinner. No warning whatsoever. He gasped, clutched his chest, and fell face down into the aspic."

"Best way to go," said Cayman, as though he had made advance arrangements for himself to go in that matter.

"Well, I'm sure it's preferable to a slow death by poisoning." Bette applied a lighter to the cigarette in her mouth. Agatha sat with her hands folded in her lap while dwelling on Bette's shrewd mind.

There was an awkward silence broken by Nellie Mamby asking Bette, "Will there be anything else?"

"What? Oh! You're going to bed."

"I thought I'd leave the clearing-up until the morning. I'm all done in."

"You poor thing. Séances are definitely not for you. I'd love to do another, but I'm sure Nydia is much too exhausted."

Nydia said, "I doubt if we'd learn any more than we've already learned."

"Good night, Mamby," said Bette. "Would you make sure all the doors and the French windows are secure before turning in?"

"Yes, Miss Bette." Mamby's eyes were on somebody else, but Bette couldn't figure out who it was. Mamby turned quickly and hurried out of the room.

"Something's bothering her," said Bette.

"Something's always bothering Nellie," said Anthea. "She's happy only when she's troubled. She's been with the family a long time. Mother hired her when Virgil was just an infant. She and Mother spoiled him rotten."

"Now, now," said Sir Roland. "You forget Virgil was a sickly child. He needed special nursing." He explained to the others while Oscar refilled his and Anthea's glasses, "During the last months of her pregnancy, Mabel came down with some strange affliction. She accused me of bringing back a strange bug from an expedition I'd been on in Ethiopia. It's possible, I suppose, but I wasn't infected with anything. At least if I was, it didn't affect me at all. Anyway, Virgil couldn't hold his food down and cried something awful day and night, and we spent a fortune on specialists, and then one day he was miraculously as good as new. And that was the end of that very awful period."

Bette asked, "Sir Roland, did you love Virgil?"

He replied staunchly, "I love all my children."

"Even when Virgil eclipsed your sun?"

"It was bound to happen sooner or later, whether it was by Virgil or some other archeologist. I always thought Agatha's Max would be the one to force me from my pedestal."

"Not Max. Never my Max. He digs for knowledge and for the joy of exploring fresh territories. He doesn't want to parade about in a spotlight. Of course, despite this, he has made a name for himself."

"Quite a jolly good name," said Sir Roland unbegrudgingly. He leaned forward with a sycophantic smile. "Of course, he doesn't have to consider making huge profits. He has a clever wife with a fortune of her own."

"I do not support my husband," said Agatha pointedly and with great dignity. "He would never permit that. Whatever my fame as a writer, Max is very much the head of our household. When he's in residence."

Cayman said suddenly, "Bette, you fascinate me."

"I do? What brought that on?"

"The way you lean forward and listen so intently. You absorb the conversations of others like a sponge."

"Well, Inspector, as an officer of the law I'm sure you learn more by listening then by talking."

"I do try, but sometimes it's difficult to learn anything from some of the gobbledygook I have to listen to."

"I'm really quite flattered you've said that," said Bette, "because I've been told listening is a great art. Especially in an actor." She indicated she needed a refill and Nayland took her glass. "One of the greatest listeners in the theater is Ethel Barrymore. I'm sure you've heard of her."

"My dear Bette, condescension does not become you. Ethel Barrymore made a great hit in London when she was but a girl. I was madly in love with her, along with half a hundred others. I almost came to blows with Winston Churchill over her," revealed Sir Roland.

"I'm a damned good listener," said Bette. Agatha was grateful she had derailed Sir Roland. "I've learned from studying Miss Barrymore. She truly listens to her fellow actors even though she's heard the words so many times, especially if she's in a long run. She concentrates on what they're saying, not just listening for her cues, and it makes for a better performance by her. Agatha, you're a very good listener, and so are you, Inspector, but of course listening is an integral part of your profession." Nayland returned with her refill. "Oh, thank you, Mr. Nayland. You're a treasure." Nayland was kept busy by Cayman and Agatha. The Wynns seemed to be nursing their drinks as though nursing them had been agreed upon earlier and rehearsed.

"I'm a good listener," said Agatha, "because I can also listen between the lines. I can tell when a woman gushing about her marvelous husband really wishes he'd end the affair he's having with her best friend. And I always know that when my editor is waxing poetic over my manuscript he bloody wants me to fix the first five chapters. Yes, listening is indeed an art, but sometimes it can be terribly dangerous. One can hear too much, or think one has heard too much. Don't you agree, Inspector?"

"I listen mostly for the slips," said Cayman. "Nayland here sometimes wonders how during an interrogation I don't find myself screaming, 'Oh, shut the hell up,' when the person I'm questioning drones on and on, seemingly saying nothing worth repeating but somewhere inadvertently giving something away."

Sir Roland asked, "And what have you heard so far that's of importance to you and probably not to us?"

Cayman replied, "I listen. But I never tell what I've heard."

"Ah! Like the Sphinx!"

Bette called out, "Mamby? Is there something else you wanted? I know you're outside the door." She explained to the others, "She has this noisy way of breathing. Haven't you noticed during all her years of service?"

Mamby appeared in the doorway. "I didn't mean to disturb you. I was just going to see to the windows in the front parlor."

"Then don't let me delay you. Your poor body must be riddled with exhaustion."

Cayman laughed and said, "I was damned right. You certainly are a good listener!"

Agatha spoke up. "What have you heard tonight, Bette?"

"Same things you did." She was lighting a cigarette, squinting when the smoke attacked her eyes.

"But we all put a different interpretation on what we've heard," insisted Agatha.

"Okay," said Bette. "I'll play. 'There's safety in numbers.'"

Nydia Tilson asked, "Did that come out of my mouth?"

Bette said, "Oh, poor Nydia. We haven't told you what you told us! How awful we are! Of course, you couldn't hear yourself speak. You were in a trance! You were, weren't you?"

"I most certainly was."

"Well, why didn't you ask us what Virgil said?"

"Because I assumed he never came through! Not one of you mentioned the fact that he had! I thought you'd all be babbling away when I came out of the trance."

Agatha said, "You will forgive us, dear. I should have spoken up at once. I'm so familiar with your séances and how eager you are to find out if you were a success or not. I think it's Virgil's murder that's preoccupying us."

Nydia had a look of satisfaction. "So we contacted Virgil! Well! Who killed him?"

"He never said," said Agatha.

"Why not?" Nydia was appalled, or seemed to be.

Cayman said with a slight touch of whimsy, "Perhaps it would have been rude to ask."

Agatha interrupted, "It was all Mabel's fault."

"What's Mabel got to do with it?"

Agatha said, "She interrupted Virgil, as she was always wont to do."

Bette looked at her wristwatch. "Unless you're all beat, I say let's go back to the table and try again!"

"I can't," said Nydia. "I'm spent." Her eyes widened. "Did Joan of Arc show up again?"

"The usual nuisance," said Agatha.

"And Renée Adorée," said Bette enthusiastically.

Nydia was bemused. "Who's that?"

"Silent-film actress. Dead, of course. She spoke on behalf of John Gilbert."

"Sounds as though it all came over in terrible confusion."

"It was quite clear to me," said Bette. "Virgil kept repeating, 'There's safety in numbers.' Well, I think he meant that since we were all together at the table and touching pinkies"— she found a smile for Cayman, who winked in return—"it would be impossible for the killer to strike again."

Anthea said angrily, "Are you implying that one of us is a murderer?"

Agatha decided to speak for Bette. "My dear Anthea, it's more than likely."

"How dare you!" Anthea looked as though she was about to be raped. "Inspector, do you suspect my father, my brother, or myself of killing Virgil?"

" 'There's safety in numbers.' "

Nydia said, "Anthea, the inspector has also invited Mamby and myself to an interrogation at Scotland Yard tomorrow. Don't be so obtuse and stop fiddling with your pearls. It seems Virgil was being poisoned slowly, and we all had the opportunity to poison him. Wasn't there a Madeleine something or other in Scotland who did in her brother in the same way? I think I rather enjoy being a murder suspect. It's a new experience for me."

Especially, Bette was thinking, if it was truly a heart attack that snuffed out your husband's life. Suddenly she was compelled to ask, "Inspector, darling, do murderers have a special look?"

"You mean, such as deep-set eyes that are much too close together? Or missing earlobes or a finger or two?" He stared at the ceiling briefly. "There was Diana Fotheringill."

"Oh, I remember her," piped up Nayland. "Very dishy she was, if I do say so myself. Murdered her husband and his three mistresses, and did a very neat job of it too. Also poison," he confided to the others.

"She was pigeon-toed," said Cayman.

"You're putting us on," said Bette. "If pigeon toes were the indication of a murderer, then prisons the world over would be bursting their walls. I played a murderer in *Bordertown*. Very nasty. I locked my drunken husband in the garage, where he sat behind the wheel of our car with the motor running. Then I went mad and confessed. It was quite a scene. I had indigestion for days from all the scenery I chewed."

"Carbon monoxide poisoning," said Agatha with relish. "What a lovely way to go. That's filed away among my little gray cells for future use."

"It's a painless way to go," said Bette. "That's what the studio doctor told me."

Oscar came out of his deep silence. "It didn't sound like Mabel."

"What didn't?" asked Anthea.

"What came out of Nydia's mouth. There was too much screeching."

"Have you forgotten?" asked Sir Roland. "Your mother was frequently given to screeching."

"I always thought it more shrill than screech."

"I certainly recognized it as your mother. She certainly gave me what for. It's not pleasant being told your offer of marriage was accepted because you were the only one available and she wanted to lose her virginity." He added solemnly, "Mabel had this awful habit of misplacing her virginity. I sometimes think I was the world's prize cuckold."

"You can console yourself that it's all now in the past," sympathized Bette.

"Not with that bloody séance to remind me! Whose idea was it, anyway, to hold the séance?"

"Mine," said Nydia. "No one forced you to participate."

"To be perfectly honest, I didn't want to participate. But then it occurred to me that to absent myself would be tantamount to a confession of guilt."

Agatha said, "With which statement, Roland, you confirm the suspicion that there is possibly a murderer among you."

"If so, it will have to be proven, won't it, Inspector?"

"That's why I'm here," said Cayman, "very busy listening."

Sir Raymond bristled. "I find being under suspicion is terribly undignified."

Bette suggested, "Why not think of it as being something special, like pheasant under glass?"

"I must say, Bette, you're given to rather strange analogies." Bette was amused by Sir Roland. She thought he'd make a fortune in Hollywood as a character actor. He could certainly give C. Aubrey Smith a run for his money, and Sir Roland's upper lip seemed stiffer than most.

Nydia said, "What's on your mind, Bette?"

"What?" Her hand was flailing about like a pinfeather caught in a strong breeze.

"You're staring at me."

"Oh, darling, quite unconsciously, I assure you. I have this habit of staring without really seeing. My mind was elsewhere, I assure you."

Nydia stated flatly, "You're skeptical about what went on at the séance."

"I question everything, Nydia. It's my Yankee upbringing. I've been known to send scriptwriters over the edge. Actually, Nydia, you should consider dividing your time between England and Hollywood. You'd be a huge success there. I'm sure Marion Davies and Mr. Hearst were quite pleased with your performance." After speaking the word 'performance,' Bette caught Agatha from a corner of an eye giving her a very strange look.

"I've no gift for prescience," said Nydia, "but somehow I agree I haven't seen the last of Hollywood." She glanced at her wristwatch. "You must forgive me, but I'm truly exhausted. I must get back to Cadogan Square, and taxis aren't all that easy to find around here at this time of night."

Agatha made a move to rise. "I'll ring one for you, dear. The number for the local cab rank is in Mamby's book in the kitchen. She's abed, so I dare invade it. Is it all right, Bette?"

"That sore point has been settled with Mamby," said Bette with a smile that reflected victory. "The kitchen is no longer off limits."

Cayman stepped in. "No need to summon a taxi, Mrs. Mallowan. Nayland, be a good chap and run Mrs. Tilson home. Then come back here for me."

Sir Roland said, "You can summon a taxi for Oscar, Anthea, and myself, if you don't mind."

Suavely and with great charm, Nayland offered to chauffeur all of them to their various destinations. He assured them the car was large enough to accommodate them comfortably. It was apparent to Bette and Agatha that Cayman had no intention of leaving as yet. Agatha started to say it was time she too retired, but Bette swiftly asked her to stay for a nightcap.

"Oh, really?" asked Agatha. "Are you sure it's not an imposition?"

"Hell, no," said Bette. "Inspector, be a dear and do the honors while I see the others to the door."

After the exchange of good nights between Bette, the Wynns, and Nydia, Cayman went to the liquor cabinet. Agatha said, "Bette should keep a bowl of fruit in this room."

"Starving for an apple?"

"Actually, no. I've been served quite a bit of food for thought tonight, as I'm sure you have too. Pour a bit more if that's my glass, I'm not too anxious to be embraced by the arms of Morpheus as yet."

"Don't tell me the séance has given you a bit of a turn," said Cayman as he brought her her drink.

"Indeed it has, but not the way you think. Is that glass for Bette? Put it on the coffee table. She seems to enjoy the sofa. Actresses like to spread out on sofas. I've learned that from the ladies who have appeared in my plays." Bette returned. "Your drink's on the coffee table, dear." She watched Cayman pour another for himself, while Bette lit an inevitable cigarette. "I find it so strange, Inspector, and I'm sure you do too."

"What's that?" Cayman sat next to Bette.

"It's strange how people involved in a murder don't believe the killer dwells among them."

"The only one who was strongly upset was Anthea Wynn," Cayman reminded them.

Said Bette, paraphrasing Shakespeare, "Perhaps the lady doth protest too much."

Cayman said, "There are times when I find that even murderers convince themselves they've committed no crime. Murder wears so many faces."

"So do murderers," said Agatha.

Bette sat forward intently. "Now come on, you two. I have a great deal of respect for both of you and I want you to level with me. Do you really believe the spirit world exists?"

"I have several times been astonished by what I have taken to be occult phenomena." Agatha sounded appropriately mysterious.

"You've witnessed manifestations? You've seen ectoplasm?" Bette's eyes were popping with curiosity.

"I think we all have at one time or another without realizing it. During the war there were many reports of ghostly manifestations in heavily shelled areas of Europe. There have been many magazine and newspaper articles. Nydia brought up Houdini. He was a fanatic about the occult, always trying to contact his mother. She was the most important person in his life. And, of course, Sherlock's creator, Conan Doyle. He left detailed instructions on how to try and get in touch with him."

"You said he wasn't terribly communicative," Bette reminded her.

"That was in this world. Perhaps for the afterworld he foresaw loneliness."

Bette giggled. "Wouldn't it be fun if we could contact him

and find he's written a whole new set of Sherlock Holmes stories?"

"I hope he's got a good agent," said Agatha dryly. "Inspector, are you too beset by skepticism?"

"I'm a born skeptic. But I learned a lot tonight. Mrs. Tilson is very, very good."

Agatha agreed. "She certainly has a gift."

Bette was at a French window looking out at the rising fog beginning to enshroud her garden. It's heavy curtain made some of the shrubbery look like tiny apparitions. Bette was thinking, Nydia does indeed have a gift, and I think it could be a very dangerous gift.

"What's out there, Bette?" asked Cayman.

"Apparitions. Manifestations." She laughed. "There's a heavy fog settling in on us. What looks like a pea-souper. Isn't that what you call them?"

Agatha said, "You know, I sometimes think that fog is a form of ectoplasm. We suffer too much fog in London. It's very dangerous to our health."

"It's very dangerous as a curtain for criminals," said Cayman. "Footpads proliferate in them."

"Footpads!" said Agatha, though not quite scoffing. "How archaic!"

Bette asked, "What kind of pads are footpads?"

Cayman elucidated, "It's a very out-of-date expression for thieves who lurk in the night using the fog to camouflage their nasty activities."

Bette placed her glass on the coffee table when she returned from the window. As she walked back slowly she asked, "They don't try climbing over protective walls, do they?"

"Now see what you've done, Inspector. You're frightening Bette!" admonished Agatha.

"No he hasn't. It takes an awful lot to frighten me. I don't believe bogies hide in dark rooms or look for intruders under my bed, though I admit there have been nights when I would have welcomed one. Why, you dear man, you're filling my glass again."

Cayman said, "Spirits are the only good accompaniment for spirits."

Agatha held up her empty glass. "As Garbo said on her entrance in *Anna Christie*"—she did a near-perfect impersonation of the Swede's voice—" 'Giff me a visky, ginger ale on the side, and don't be stingy, baby.' "

Bette was delighted. "Agatha, that's very, very good! You have a wonderful ear! You've caught her perfectly."

Agatha demurred. "No I haven't. I merely created a passable illusion."

"Yes. That's what you've done. You've created a passable illusion. I think we've had quite a bit of that tonight."

9

"So we're back to Nydia," said Agatha.

"We've never left. Why do you think I wanted you two to stay on after the others left?"

"You let Nydia get away."

"It's not as though we've seen the last of her. And I certainly don't want to. I like Nydia very much. She's become a wonderful friend. But one can question certain activities of friends, can't one?

"Most assuredly," agreed Agatha. "I'm always questioning certain peccadilloes of my acquaintances and often wish I hadn't. You heard things tonight the way I did and the way the inspector did, but we heard them differently from each other. That is to say, we interpret what we've heard differently."

Bette sat on an ottoman next to Agatha. "Listen, you two. We have a medium in Hollywood who's made so much money, he lives in a fantastic mansion in Laurel Canyon, and by the way, it's not too far from the old Houdini estate. This man is in my opinion a complete charlatan, but he does one thing that perhaps only men of the cloth can do, especially for the weak-minded: he gives comfort. His clientele are largely widows of all denominations and of all walks of Los Angeles life. I've sat in on a few of his séances because Warners wanted

130

me to do a movie with Warren William, him as a medium and me as his associate. Rotten script. Never got made. Anyway, he knew I was a skeptic and he was absolutely delighted to accept the challenge. Mind you, he used none of the cliché appurtenances one is conditioned to expect from spiritualists. No tambourines, no horns tooting and the rest of that razzmatazz. But each time I was there, he told someone at the table something they claimed was genuine. I have to admit it was absolutely uncanny. He even got me a message from one of my late aunts, but anybody can read up on me in my studio biography." She was chain smoking, just warming up to her subject. "But there was a woman one time who was absolutely dying of bereavement. I really mean that. She was inconsolable over the loss of her only son in an automobile accident. I'd been at two sessions with her and both times she held conversations with what she presumed was her son. And she never once denied a thing he said or claimed to have happened!" She stared from one to the other as though expecting a challenge. "Well? What have you to say to that?"

Agatha looked like a wise old owl. "I have this to say. You said she held conversations with what she presumed was her son. Well, that's exactly what she did. She presumed. She had every intention of speaking with her son, and as far as she was concerned, it was her son with whom she was conversing. Of course, the son spoke in a ghostly whisper or whatever passes for a ghost's voice."

"Come to think of it, you're right."

"Of course I'm right," agreed Agatha, trying not to sound too smug. "Tell me this, Bette. The room in which he conducts his séances, is it very heavily draped with curtains that obscure the walls?"

"You've been there."

"I have not. It's the same setting for every séance I have ever participated in, except for Nydia's."

"Right!" exclaimed Bette. "No curtains."

Cayman finally spoke. "I don't think Mrs. Tilson needs to

create an illusion, especially when she's quite confident she knows what she's talking about. And I'm quite positive she is well versed in the Wynn family."

"Yes. Of course. Agatha, why the curtains?"

"To create an occult illusion. The curtains were certainly very dark and very velvet."

"Very, very on both counts."

"You see, Bette, the curtains can also be used to obscure an accomplice or two who do the voices the spiritualist is unable to perfect. There's one spiritualist in Brighton who is a mute, yet when he conducts a séance, he articulates miraculously."

"I know the answer to that one," said Bette. "Ventriloquism."

"Clever," said Agatha. "You have a very good deductive mind."

Bette said slowly, "So, in other words, people hear what they want to hear, despite the fact that it's just the power of suggestion."

"It's the same with *obeah*," said Agatha.

"What in God's name is that?"

"Voodoo. Black magic. Witch doctors."

"You mean the casting of spells and the burning of the intended victim's hair and nail parings?"

"It's very effective, my dear. It frightens the hell out of illiterates and innocents in Negro nations, and they bring about their own deaths. All due to the power of suggestion. The fear of the unknown. When you were starting out in the theater and had to audition, didn't you have palpitations, weren't you frightened of rejection, weren't you weak in the knees—"

"But never weak in the head. Sorry, Agatha, but I was a very determined neophyte. What I lacked in looks and polish I made up for with tenacity and determination. Agatha, I was a killer."

And I suspect you still are, thought Cayman, but I'm not going to say so if I ever expect to see this undernourished flirtation develop into something of much greater interest and impact.

Agatha was speaking. "You know, I've known Nydia for a great many years. Max was Ogden's friend at university, and although Max has never admitted it, I think Ogden assisted in financing Max's earliest forays into archeology. I am positive Nydia believes in what she does as a medium. Oh, I think she does do a bit of shading and highlighting here and there. That actress person tonight, what was her name?"

"Renée Adorée." Bette was dying for another drink but didn't want her guests to suspect she had a problem with alcohol, which she didn't. Cayman, bless him, thought Bette, offered to do the honors with the refills.

"Exactly. Yes. Renée Adorée. Wherever do you suppose she dredged her up from?"

"I've seen movie magazines in Nydia's flat. And she's just returned from Hollywood and a séance for Marion Davies. I'm sure she pulled the Renée Adorée and John Gilbert combination on them. I would think our Nydia did a great deal of reading and research about Hollywood before conducting her session there."

"Yes, Nydia has a very inquisitive mind. Shortly after we met, she got a bit brave and started to ask questions about Archibald, my first husband. He was with the Royal Air Force and therefore a bit flighty. He was also a cad and a scoundrel, but that's not important now, though God knows . . ." She stopped. "And what God knows shall be strictly between Him and me. Anyway, I didn't tell her very much and she backed off from me, but that didn't stop her from pursuing others. Then, when that Indian was impressed by her at the Houdini session, there was no stopping our Nydia. She took off like a rocket and started at the top with the wealthy muck-amucks of Mayfair. And soon she was invited to Buckingham Palace by Queen Mary. She slowed down briefly after Ogden's sudden and unexpected death."

"Face in the aspic," reminded Bette.

"He loathed aspic. Maybe the sight of it is what done him in. Once she realized how much wealth Ogden had possessed and had passed on to her, Nydia blossomed. She was now a very rich medium, which of course is very rare." Bette and Cayman exchanged warm glances as he handed her her drink and then gave Agatha hers. "Nydia began to get even better. She took chances, such as once conjuring up what was supposed to be the spirit of Genghis Khan, and she knocked me for a loop—her Chinese was *that* good. It turned out in a misspent moment in her youth she had trafficked with a young Chinese juggler she met when she was doing music halls, and when he disappeared back to China he left her with little but a smattering of Mandarin."

"I knew it!" said Bette. "She did music halls! Isn't that what you said?"

"Well, it's a fact. She told me so ages ago."

"I suspected there was an actress hiding in the woodpile. And she's a pretty good mimic too, isn't she?"

"She was right on the nose with Virgil, though for my taste I thought she overdid Mabel a bit. Of course, the Renée Adorée could have been any Frenchwoman sitting behind the cash register of a Montparnasse café. You have to admit, Bette, Nydia carries it off brilliantly, and she does suffuse the show with some charming bits of humor. Don't you agree?"

"Oh, sure. But oh boy, was she trying to tell us a lot with Mabel's outburst and Virgil's 'There's safety in numbers.' Come on, Inspector, impress us with a theory. It's quite obvious, or I think it's quite obvious, that Nydia suspects Virgil's murder was the work of more than one person."

"You mean a conspiracy," said Cayman. Bette nodded. "Those things are awfully hard to prove."

"Why?" asked Bette with her arms folded.

"Mostly because one can be strangled by a tissue of lies. Before you can unravel the threads and get to the core, which is the truth, you have very little with which to make an accusation that will stick. No, I think there's a single murderer behind Virgil's death."

"What about Mabel?" Bette was in her element, and Agatha was having a whale of a time watching her and listening to her. Truly a sly puss.

"What about her?"

"Who murdered Mabel?"

"She overdosed on a sleeping draught."

Bette turned to Agatha. "Was Mabel a poor sleeper?"

"I knew you'd guess."

"So she took sleeping draughts to knock herself out." Her voice went up an octave. "Very easily doctored! Except that in her case, unlike Virgil's, she got hers in one fatal dose."

"Mabel had cancer. Inoperable." Agatha waited to see what Bette would do with that bombshell.

Bette's eyes narrowed. "Agatha Christie, don't try to trip me up. She was fed her death, and now I suspect she knew what she was getting, and obviously so suspects Nydia. All that improvisation about its not being bitter and tasting better than she thought, and how she wasn't afraid of Death, especially if he looked like Freddie March. Well, just go ask Freddie's wife, Florence Eldridge, what kind of death her husband looks like after returning from some all-night session with the many aspiring actresses he seduces. Mabel was murdered, and whether or not she was a party to her own fate, I still call it murder. Don't you, Inspector?"

"You might have something there." Bette heard encouragement and her winning smile convinced him he'd scored important points. "It certainly bears consideration."

"Of course it does!" said Bette with infectious enthusiasm. "Oh, damn! Why did we let Nydia slip through our fingers? I'm sure she suspects more than she let on tonight. Agatha, what's the truth about Nydia and Virgil? Were they really in love or were they going through the motions? Forgive me, but

I've never had any reason to associate the British with intense passion."

"Have you never had an affair with an Englishman?" asked Agatha. She might as well have been asking if she'd ever sampled jellied eels.

"No. Not really. Dear old George Arliss seemed to have a restrained interest in me, but I'd hardly call it passion."

"My dear girl," said Agatha with a sly eye towards Cayman, "you must give it a try."

Bette laughed. "I'll try anything once. Now, come on, you two, let's stay with Virgil and Nydia. Agatha, you and Nydia have been confidantes for years."

" 'Confidantes' is a bit of an overstatement. We certainly gossip a great deal and see a flick or attend the theater together, but I think most of our innermost secrets remain just that, innermost. If you're wondering whether she confided in me about her feelings about Virgil, I have every reason to believe Nydia kept a cool head where he was concerned. Keep in mind, Mabel was still among the living then and plotting and scheming her salons. Virgil was the bellwether of those gatherings. It was his sudden fame that gave Mabel the impetus to carve her way to the top of the social stratosphere. She hadn't the international reputation enjoyed by Syrie Maugham and your Elsa Maxwell, but she had their kind of drive and determination. When Mabel was beginning her onslaught, Ogden and Nydia were a desirable couple. Ogden's wealth kept him in the public eye. He was a very generous man and he gave his support to a variety of charities. He was awfully good to wayward girls."

"I'll bet," interjected Bette after exhaling an enchanting smoke ring.

Agatha sighed. "I left myself open to that one. Actually, Ogden was very modest and self-effacing. He left the flamboyance to Nydia. When he met her, she'd done very well for herself as Cecily in Oscar Wilde's *The Importance of Being Earnest*. It put her on the theatrical map as someone to keep a favorable eye on. Men pursued her shamelessly, and just as shamelessly she encouraged them. She was very wise, however, to concentrate most of her encouragement on Ogden. He was very, very wealthy and, in his way, rather attractive. Max knew Ogden, as I've already told you, and he asked me to have the couple around to Sunday dinner. Well, Nydia and I took to each other immediately. She had learned I was interested in amateur theatricals and she knew I'd had some success with my plays, and of course I'm sure it occurred to her I'd be writing others and there might be one with a part suitable for her. She invited us to see her in *Earnest*, and she was really quite good." She said to Cayman, "I usually dread seeing a friend in a play, because if they're not very good, what do you say to them when you go backstage afterwards? Dear Estelle Winwood went to see Gladys Cooper in something perfectly awful and almost went berserk wracking her brain for something complimentary. When she got to her dressing room Gladys trumpeted, 'Well? What did you think?' Estelle looked at Gladys and was inspired to say, 'My dear, throughout the play I kept wishing you were sitting beside me.' In Nydia's case, I could tell her quite happily that she was a very gifted young actress. When Ogden asked her to marry him, Nydia did come to me for advice. He wanted her to give up acting. A tough decision for what you would call a hot young property to make. She was truly torn. Her profession or Ogden's millions."

"Not Ogden the man?" asked Bette.

"I'm with you, Bette. I prefer to think she considered the man before she considered the millions."

"You advised her to marry him, I take it."

"In a way I did. I told her, or rather reminded her, that she wouldn't be young forever. And money never ages."

"Good for you! And so they were married." Bette smiled at Cayman. Her glass was empty again, and it needed refilling, as did her heart. She knew he could refill her glass, but in the matter of the heart, his credentials were questionable.

"Indeed, they were married and to all intents and purposes lived happily ever after." She said to Bette, "You believe in happy endings?"

Bette replied with an edge to her voice, "When I want a happy ending, I go to a funeral."

Agatha chuckled. "Ogden died much too soon. Still a young man. And now spiritualism had entered Nydia's world and in its way filled the void I think she suffered after abandoning her career. There were Mabel's weekly salons."

Bette asked as Cayman, stifling a yawn, did the honors with the liquor again, "That's where she met Virgil?"

"Indeed."

"And they were attracted to each other?"

"I would be more apt to say Virgil was attracted to Nydia. Nydia was a faithful wife, Bette. She really cared for Ogden, and of course Ogden was absolutely dotty about her." She went quiet, as though wondering if she should share any further information.

Cayman said, "This sudden quiet is deafening."

"While hearing myself talk, I found my thoughts wandering in another direction."

"Come on, Agatha. Don't hold out. It might help the inspector formulate some answers. It's late, and I'm sure he's got a lot on his plate in the morning."

"Virgil suddenly appeared at Nydia's door to kindly see if she needed any help with coping. Funeral arrangements, all that. Nydia has no family. She's very alone. And was even more alone in Cadogan Square now that Ogden was laid out elsewhere, in the mortuary. Max and I of course pitched in. Nydia made overuse of my shoulder and seemed never to stop crying. And in the face of a woman's tears Max becomes paralyzed. So Virgil took charge, and, I must say, most impressively. In no time at all, he had the husband consigned to the family vault. He had notified Ogden's solicitor, and Nydia learned she was Ogden's sole heir, with wealth she had never imagined possessing. I mean that Ogden's wealth could have been spelled out in neon lights. I might add, she has invested very wisely, thanks to my broker."

"So now begins the romance between Nydia and Virgil," said Cayman.

Bette said, "I have a feeling we could now use some orchestral accompaniment."

"Theirs was a rough beginning," said Agatha gravely. "In the first place, a woman so freshly widowed must exercise discretion in her relationships with the opposite sex or be doomed to a most distressing reputation. Nydia is no fool and was no fool. She was polite but for the most part kept Virgil at arm's length. If they were to dine in public, I or someone else accompanied them. What went on in the privacy of Nydia's apartment I cannot attest to."

"And you couldn't care less," added Bette.

"Like hell I couldn't! I was dying to know what was going on. My dear, remember, I adore gossip and I'm only human. Full marks for myself that I didn't press Nydia, though it pained me not to. But I sensed the growing intimacy and so did the Wynn women. Anthea behaved like a complete fool. Tantrums. Threats. She was too terrible. I got all this second-hand from Sir Roland, who, contrary to his insistence that he loved all his children, was bored senseless by them, though not so much by Virgil. At least with him he could share a mummy or two over a glass of port at the Club."

"And how did Mabel behave?" Bette's voice was growing hoarse. Scotch whisky and cigarettes were beginning to take their toll.

"Mabel was a bit subtler then Anthea, which wasn't difficult, as, in my experience, Anthea has never been subtle. What Mabel did was cruel. She cut Nydia from her guest list. Her excuse was she had a plethora of single women. Nydia seemed not to mind. She spent most Sundays with us. I never accepted Mabel's invitations, much to Max's joy. He couldn't stand her."

Bette asked, "What were your thoughts when Mabel died?"

" 'Toodle-oo, dearie. Have a nice trip.' " The three blended into laughter. "Oh, aren't I awful! I had nothing against Mabel. I just thought she was a silly, rich woman given to dropping names all over the place. Though I gather she did set a good table."

"Did you know she was terminally ill?" asked Cayman.

"I didn't hear it directly from anyone. Though the salons went from one a week to one every two weeks and then to one a month, and then they evanesced. And then there was her obituary in the *Times*, with the explanation 'death by misadventure.' Isn't that a divine expression, Bette? 'Death by misadventure'!"

"Oh, God, it must be the whisky! I thought 'Adventure' was some woman's name! 'Miss Adventure'!" They shared a laugh again.

"How do they put it in America?" asked Agatha.

"They come right out with it. Suicide by overdose or self-inflicted gunshot wound or she took a dive off the roof. We don't pussyfoot around with those things. And I suppose because no foul play was suspected, there was no autopsy."

"Not that I know of," replied Agatha. "Of course the inspector could find out if he were so inclined."

"I doubt if there was an autopsy. And I'm not about to look into having her body exhumed until I can prove for sure that she met with foul play. And that could be very, very tricky this late in the game."

"Friends," said Bette, a faraway look in her eyes, "I wonder if Nellie Mamby knew what was going on." She snapped her finger. "I'll bet you she knew and knows a hell of a lot more than she's willing to admit."

"Or ever will admit," said Agatha.

"She wasn't very happy with the séance," said Betty. "All that heavy breathing of hers, I daresay, was hardly due to any bubbling passion. Agatha, was she fond of Mabel?"

"I would say she was. She lasted a long time in her employ.

And she continued as part of the household. Because of the salons, Mamby was practically a celebrity in her own right. She was deared and darlinged to near-paralyzation by a lot of Mabel's celebrities. Noel Coward invited her to a matinee of *Cavalcade*, and Sir Thomas Beecham asked her to the Albert Hall on at least two occasions I heard about."

Bette asked eagerly, "Could there have been any hanky-panky?"

"With Noel? I'm sure that if there were, he wasn't aware of it. As for Thomas . . . Oh, really, Bette. You've seen Mamby! How could you even suggest hanky-panky and Mamby in the same breath?"

Bette was on her feet and pacing, semaphoring no one in particular with her overactive hand holding its smoking cigarette. "Agatha, for a woman of the world you astonish me with your naiveté."

Agatha said firmly, "I am *not* a woman of the world and have never professed to be. I admit to being naive about a great many things, but to picture Mamby as the object of anybody's passion is like asking me to insist the moon is made of green cheese."

"Ladies! Lower your voices!" cautioned Cayman. "She might hear you and come flying in to her own defense!"

"Don't be ridiculous," said Bette, emphasizing her words with a dismissing gesture of her hand. "She's all the way in the back of the house dead asleep and probably uttering unappetizing little wheezes. Agatha, you wouldn't believe the physiognomies of some of the wives and husbands of our stars. I mean, look at Jean Harlow!"

"Oh, I so enjoy looking at Jean Harlow," said Cayman enthusiastically.

"Her second husband, Paul Bern, the one who supposedly committed suicide, was hardly an Adonis. He looked like a pants presser! Paul Muni's wife is a sweet pain the backside, but she'd never stop traffic unless she were in an accident. The man I just dismissed from my life is attractive enough but not in his BVDs. Agatha, one can never predict what people will go for in the opposite sex."

"Bette," said Cayman.

"Yes?"

"The door is chiming."

"So it is. Maybe it's Nydia coming back, having caught a second wind!"

Cayman said, "I prefer to think it's Nayland come to fetch me."

"Oh, of course. I'd forgotten Nayland." She hurried out.

"Nayland's quite a nice chap. Not all that memorable, but at the same time not all that forgettable. He's awfully good at his job, but I never tell him, as it might spoil him."

"She's quite clever, isn't she?"

"You mean Bette?"

"I don't mean Marie of Rumania."

"She's got quite a head on her shoulders. I admire the interior as much as I do the exterior."

"How lucky you are. Having it both ways."

"I haven't had it any way, as yet."

"I suppose you're also wondering what she was after, implicating Nellie Mamby."

"Oh? Do you consider that implicating? I suppose you could, couldn't you? Right now I'm too tired. I'll give it some thought tomorrow."

"It's already tomorrow," said Bette as she returned, followed by Nayland.

"Poor chap," said Cayman to Nayland. "You look all in."

"Well, sir, it was quite a trip!"

"He could use a whisky!" exclaimed Bette.

"Dear girl," said Agatha, "I believe we've all had more than enough to drink for one evening!"

"Oh, look at poor Mr. Nayland. I can tell he's feeling deprived." Cayman wearily went to the liquor cabinet and poured four drinks. He had looked at his wristwatch, and it was almost midnight. His first interrogation was Nellie Mamby at nine o'clock. And then the other suspects at two-hour intervals. And then there was the knife that had been plunged into the back of Virgil's mouth. That had to be found, though he was sure it was clean of any fingerprints. He'd need a description of the weapon from Sir Roland.

"Inspector," cried Bette, rousing Cayman from his momentary reverie, "you've got to hear this!"

"Coming," he replied, placing the four drinks on a tray and walking slowly as he did a balancing act. "Much ado about something in the car, Nayland? I did hope there would be, which is why I didn't want Mrs. Mallowan to phone for a taxi."

"I suspected you were up to something. Don't think you put anything over on me!" said Bette.

"I wasn't trying to put anything over on you. I was trying to put something over on them." He distributed the drinks. "It was a long shot. I thought there was the danger they'd be more cautious with a detective at the wheel. I had a strong feeling that if I could get Nydia cornered by the Wynns there'd be a great kerfuffle about the séance."

"Indeed there was," said Nayland, taking a healthy swig from his glass and then suddenly glowing as the alcohol charged through his veins.

"Come on, Nayland," coaxed Cayman. "Let's hear it."

"Anthea Wynn started it. Much whining and weeping about Virgil and who could have been feeding him the poison, followed by Oscar wondering who stabbed Virgil, followed by Sir Roland calling Nydia an unmitigated bitch. And how dare she imply the family had acted in concert, with that bit about 'There's safety in numbers.' Nydia herself had an axe to grind where Virgil was concerned. Something about him giving Nydia bad advice on some investments."

"That's nonsense," said Agatha. "I've told you, Nydia is looked after by my broker, and he's the ace of spades. And why would Virgil give anyone any tips on the stock market?

He knew nothing about the market. Mabel was a whiz at investments. She always had tips. She was always soliciting them and getting them. And besides, if for some unbelievable reason it's true, if Nydia lost anything in the market, unless it was a million or so, she would have plenty left. And by plenty, I mean she's loaded. I know she has a safety-deposit box that is an El Dorado of expensive jewelry."

"I'm sorry, Mrs. Mallowan, but I'm only repeating what I overheard," said Nayland, wondering if he dared do an Oliver Twist and ask for more whisky.

"Of course you are. And quite admirably. Inspector, he is indeed quite good at his job. Please go on, Mr. Nayland." Agatha was beaming.

"Mrs. Tilson then gave the three of them what for. Calling them ungrateful wretches. Saying how often she had interceded with brother Virgil to increase their allowances, and"—he hesitated, and Cayman prodded him to continue— "now that Virgil's dead and they come into the money, will Anthea remember to repay the debts she owes Mrs. Tilson?"

Agatha said brightly, "How nice of Nydia. I never knew she was helping Anthea financially."

"She was helping all of them financially," said Nayland. "She ticked the other two off in turn, by which time we were at her house and she got out of the car, thanked me very much, and then slammed the door and marched off in what I suppose was a huff."

"What did the others say when they were left to themselves?" urged Cayman.

Nayland exhaled. "They weren't very kind about Mrs. Tilson."

"No discussion of Virgil Wynn's murder?" asked Cayman.

"Only that Anthea Wynn asked her father how soon the will was to be read. And he said, 'As soon as is decently possible.' And then I dropped him off. I must say, he sounded a bit curt with his good nights, but he was quite civil to me.

In fact, he reached into his pocket, presumably for a coin, but I told him quickly that Scotland Yard was quite generous."

Cayman groaned. "Nayland, you bloody liar. That's the sort of thing that could get around and then we'll never see a rise in pay."

Bette asked greedily, "Anthea and Oscar. What went on after you dumped their father?"

"It's rather interesting. Anthea started to say something about the servant . . ."

"Mamby," said Bette.

"But through the rearview mirror I could see her brother point a finger at me by way of cautioning her to shut up. So, I suppose for want of anything better to do, she started crying again. I suppose it's not my place to say, but I found her a bit tiresome."

"Well," said Cayman, "I shall try to do better with today's interrogations. And now I insist we depart and that Bette go up to bed. Mrs. Mallowan, may I have the pleasure of seeing you home?"

"Thank you, but that won't be necessary. There's a gate in the fence in the back garden and I'll be in my home before you can say, 'Bob's your uncle.' " She told Bette she'd phone around ten and left through the French window. Bette saw the policemen to the front door and promised Cayman she'd really get a good night's rest. She knew she needed it. A few minutes later, after dousing the lights in the drawing room, she slowly made her way upstairs, deep in thought.

In the garden, Agatha noticed a light beaming under a curtain from what she knew was Nellie Mamby's room. Perhaps Mamby had fallen asleep leaving the light on. Agatha continued on to her house as the hated fog was closing in on her. There was so much for her to think about.

Within a few minutes, Agatha was seated in her kitchen warming her feet at the electric fire and munching an apple. She was occupied with thinking about Nydia. Still waters were supposed to run deep, but this couldn't pertain to Nydia, as Nydia was rarely ever still. Her personality could be overpowering and there were times when she knew how to play the shrinking violet. Agatha had seen how well she could underplay as an actress. Agatha recalled Nydia telling her that Edith Evans had advised her, 'Less is more.' But as a spiritualist, Nydia could come close to giving her hand away; Agatha thought she had done so tonight by advising, 'There's safety in numbers.'

Did all the Wynns so loathe Virgil that they united to murder him? Which one of them had read up on poisons? Why, damn it all, one or the other of them were always poking about in my library. And I certainly have the best books on poison! She put the apple aside and pondered. Would that make me an accessory to the crime? Inspector Cayman likes me. Should the matter come up, I'm sure he'll be a dear and turn a blind eye and a deaf ear to it.

The subject of Nellie Mamby pushed thoughts of the Wynns aside with little effort. Agatha never had liked the housekeeper and she was a dreadful cook. All that boiled mutton and those overcooked vegetables, not to mention her unspeakable and inedible fruit tarts. Nellie had had, at one time or another, the ear of each member of the family, Mabel for sure and probably Anthea too. Anthea was always unburdening herself of things that mostly didn't require unburdening. If only her mind were as sharp as her features. Blank mind, hence blank verse. Had the fates been conspiring against Mabel and Roland, saddling them with those three unfortunate children? Perhaps 'unfortunate' was the wrong adjective for Virgil. He at least acquired fame and wealth, both of which, unfortunately, were no longer of any use to him.

Who gets the money? The house and grounds? The artifacts? And had he remembered Nydia for old times' sake? Or, she now wondered, did he too owe Nydia? Her thoughts deepened and she began to feel that those thoughts were getting her in deep over her head. Could Nydia possibly be in secret possession of a portion of the contraband artifacts? Agatha knew of one safety-deposit box, because she'd been with Nydia when Nydia needed a certain necklace. Nydia could be renting others if necessary, an entire bank of them. The officer in charge of the vault at the bank had fallen all over himself at the sight of her.

Wearily, Agatha raised herself from the chair and stretched. She turned off the electric fire and wended her way upstairs to her bedroom. Her windows faced those of what was now Bette's suite. Strange. Her lights are still on. Probably too keyed up from the night's activities. Her adrenaline must be pumping away.

Bette's adrenaline was indeed pumping away. She had heard a door slam downstairs as she was about to undress. She ran into the hall and cried out, "Who's there? Mamby, is that you?" Receiving no reply, she hurried back into her suite and grabbed a poker from the fireplace. With a good grip on it, she went back to the hall, found the switch that controlled both the upper and lower halls, and flooded them with light. Slowly she decended the stairs. She could see a light near the kitchen door. But it was a reflection from the basement. The basement door was ajar and the lights were on. Bette pulled the door wider.

"Who's down there?"

She considered going to Mamby's room and rousing her. After all, "There's safety in numbers." Bette called out again, "Whoever's down there, I've got a gun. Come up with your hands raised above your head! I'll count to three. One! Two! *Three!*" No one appeared. Oh, the hell with it, thought Bette. We Warner Brothers leading ladies are made of sterner stuff. Slowly she made her way down the basement stairs. At this hour of the night, some of the statuary took on a look of scary menace. But Bette didn't turn tail and hurry back up. She continued descending until she was standing just a few feet away from one of the mummies. She stood stock still and listened. She heard nothing. She advanced a few feet farther into the basement, the poker held high over her head, poised to strike.

She thought, There may be no one down here now, but someone has been here. Some items she remembered as having been neatly placed had been moved. She continued moving slowly. Just ahead was the shallow grave.

A hand protruded from the grave. A human hand. A woman's hand. Bette's heart was beating wildly. She craved a cigarette. She moved like a sleepwalker. She stared into the grave. The body had a knife plunged into its heart, an ancient relic.

Bette would never forget the look of horror on Nellie Mamby's twisted face. Bette did what was appropriate. She screamed.

10

AGATHA RESPONDED TO BETTE'S CRIES OF HELP from the French window in the drawing room like a beagle sent to retrieve a grouse. She had not yet undressed, so she was at Bette's side in almost no time at all. Bette still clutched the poker as she drew Agatha into the house. "She's in the basement. She's been stabbed in the chest. Mamby's been murdered." Agatha said nothing. She hurried to the basement, Bette in her wake. In the basement, Agatha stared at Mamby's face and then at the weapon protruding from her chest.

"Looks like the same one that stabbed Virgil. It had been on his desk. Remember? It was used as a paper cutter. Well, we weren't wrong about the murderer hiding the weapon down here. The killer knew exactly where to find it. We must go back up and phone the inspector. I'm sure Nayland drove them back to Scotland Yard."

Agatha was right. Cayman rounded up the coroner and four detectives on night duty, and they made tracks hastily back to the scene of the crimes. "Poor Miss Davis," commented Nayland, his tires screeching as they rounded a corner. "She's having quite an initiation into the Wynn house."

"I'm sure she's enjoying every moment of the melodrama." Tires screeched again. "There's a good chap, Nayland. Taking us hell bent for leather isn't all that necessary. Nellie Mamby's not going anyplace." He said to Angus MacDougal, the coroner, who sat in the back with two detectives, "Fortunate you were working late tonight."

MacDougal said through slightly clenched teeth, "Fortunate my Aunt Tootsie. The corpses are stacking up. There's an epidemic of homicides and I'm short of staff. I wish you'd put in a word with the chief that I could use a few extra hands. I mean, after all, the chef at Fouquet's has a *sous-chef* and a *salade-chef*."

Cayman asked, "Why in the world do you need chefs?"

"Oh, Howard, don't be so dense!" snapped MacDougal.

Lloyd Nayland said, "I hope Miss Davis is well stocked with whisky. I sense a long night ahead."

Cayman sighed and said, "I'll be able to sleep an extra hour or so later. My first appointment has just been canceled."

"I'm beginning to wonder if I might be an incipient alcoholic," said Bette from the sofa in the drawing room as Agatha refilled their glasses. She poured with a generous hand. She knew she herself could never be an alcoholic. She had too healthy an appetite, and alcoholics eat very little. She told Bette as much and Bette agreed.

"I never stop eating," admitted Bette. "It's nerves."

"My dear, yours are made of steel." She gave Bette a glass and held tightly to her own. "What bravery! Investigating the basement on your own! The killer might still have been down there!"

"I did have the poker with which to defend myself. Oh, God! That look on Mamby's face."

"Not terribly pleasant at all, considering she was homely to begin with."

"Her sister should be notified. The one she said she visited."

"All in good time. You poor dear. All this on your first day in the house! Two corpses!"

Bette said with irony, "My cup runneth over. And what's worse, to lose my housekeeper!"

"You'll have no trouble finding another," comforted Agatha. "I'll phone an agency in the morning, and within an hour you'll have a dozen lined up in the street waiting to be interviewed. This dreadful depression."

"Right. Will it never end?"

"What we need is a gigantic international conflagration. Wars always end depressions. Even though they're so depressing."

"Do you think there's a war on the horizon?"

"I'm afraid so. There are several saber rattlers on the Continent thirsting for power." Her head shot up. "Ah! Do you hear it? My favorite melody. A police siren!"

"Having phoned the others, do you suppose they'll be converging on the house?" Bette had little appetite for the Wynn family again. What experience she had earlier had of them had left a sour taste. Agatha didn't tell her there was one member of the family she hadn't reached or else who was not answering the phone because of the hour. Agatha had let it ring extendedly before giving up.

"If only to show their concern about Mamby's death. After all, she was like one of the family. Greedy."

"Oh, Agatha," chuckled Bette. "Is greed known to be contagious?"

"In my experience, most certainly. Look at my country. Gobbling up countries all over the world and strange little islands. Whatever the hell do we need with Bermuda?" The siren was drawing closer. "And what about your greedy American robber barons? And those munitions people in Europe? Greed is a dreadful disease."

"You're not greedy."

"I don't have to be. I'm very successful. I earn a lot of money, so there's no need for me to be envious or covetous."

"Well, *I'm* not greedy. I just want what's rightfully mine, especially some really good and meaty parts. You know, I think all this would make a perfectly swell movie."

"All what?"

"The murders. Here in the house."

"And what part would you play?"

"Nydia, of course! It's the meatiest. The showiest."

"Yes, it is, isn't it?" Bette didn't hear her. She was hurrying to answer the door. Agatha stared into her glass, but it was a poor substitute for a crystal ball. Virgil dead. Mamby dead. Who else, she wondered, needed to be eliminated? Perhaps no one else. She wasn't too sure, and this troubled her. She pulled herself together and smiled as Bette returned with Cayman and Nayland in tow.

"I sent Mr. MacDougal down to the basement," Bette announced gaily. "No need to dawdle and waste time. Right, Inspector?"

"Young woman," he said sternly, "this may be your house—"

"Borrowed," interjected Bette.

"—but it's my investigation. Nayland, have a look round in the basement. There's plenty of dust down there. There might be fingerprints. Certainly footprints."

As Nayland hurried out, cursing Cayman for his haste, which was losing Nayland a glass of liquor, Bette said to Cayman, "You mustn't be cross with me. I too could have been murdered."

Cayman considered that and agreed. "Except that I'm of the opinion that you're not so easily disposed of."

"My dear Inspector," said Bette, pouring him a drink while ignoring his protestation that he couldn't drink while on a case, "I'm the one who usually does the disposing. And forget about your archaic rules. You need a drink to steady your nerves."

"My nerves do not need steadying. They need a rest." He accepted the glass from Bette with gratitude. "Now, tell me what happened." He waited while she lit a cigarette.

She spoke succinctly and with easy clarity, clipping her words as was her wont, flailing her hands, pacing the floor, and overdramatizing at every opportunity, starting with hearing the door slam.

"Which door?" asked Cayman.

"How should I know?" replied Bette with a shrug of annoyance at being interrupted. "I was upstairs and the noise came from downstairs, and I'm not psychic. I would assume it was the front door, the killer making tracks out of here. Or maybe a door was slammed to attract my attention. Shall I continue, or do you prefer to continue dwelling on doors being slammed?"

"Sorry if I interrupt you from time to time, but it's part of my job."

"It's quite all right. I'm a movie star. I'm quite used to short takes. But next time you interrupt, try telling, 'Cut.' I'm quite used to that and it's less unnerving. Where was I?"

"Door slammed," said Agatha, sounding slightly bored.

"I shouted, 'Who's there,' and got no reply. Then I yelled Mamby's name and got no reply. We now understand why. This I was doing from the hall outside my suite. I ran back and got a poker from the fireplace."

"Very wise," said Cayman.

"You didn't say, 'Cut,' " said Bette sternly.

"Oops. Sorry." He winked at Agatha

"I descended with caution and thought there was a light coming from the kitchen, perhaps Mamby warming up some milk because she couldn't sleep. Well, I was quite wrong. It was coming from the basement, the door being ajar." She was facing away from them and paused, spun around, hands on her hips, and said defiantly, "I wasn't afraid, believe me I wasn't. I got terribly dramatic and shouted down to the basement that whoever was down there had better come up with their hands above their heads, as I had a gun."

"Cut. Good show."

"Oh, thank you, Inspector. I'm glad you're enjoying it."

Cayman realized he was at a Mexican stand-off and decided to hold his tongue until she declared she had nothing further to tell him. He folded his arms, crossed his legs, and sat back, while willing himself not to fall asleep.

"So I decided, The hell with it. I'll go down and have a look around. So down I went, and I will admit, even though the lights were on, that it was very, very spooky. I did notice that a few things I had remarked about earlier had been moved."

"Cut. As though someone might have been there to per-haps remove them."

"Very definitely. Agatha? You're very quiet."

"The spotlight is on you, dear. I'm busy absorbing every one of your words."

"Anyway, I could now see the shallow grave and I saw a hand sticking out. I recognized that it was a woman's hand. I suppose I should have gotten the hell out of there right then and there, but I was hypnotized. I wasn't sure at first who it was."

"Cut. It might have been me," offered Agatha.

"Oh? I never thought about that! I assumed you were in your kitchen having your last apple of the day."

"Quite right. It was sour. I didn't finish it. Do continue."

"There's not much more to tell. I moved closer, not even considering that the murderer might still be in the basement."

"Cut. Very brave of you." Cayman unfolded his arms and retrieved his drink from the end table next to him. He very definitely needed it.

"How nice of you to say that. So I looked into the grave, and there was Nellie Mamby with a dagger, an ancient relic, projecting from her chest. She looked awful."

"Cut. To be expected, in her condition." He took a deep swig.

"You don't have to say 'Cut' anymore. I'm finished. Are you going down to have a look at Mamby?"

"Why? I remember what she looks like. MacDougal and Nayland are seeing to things and they're quite capable. I have some other detectives waiting outside in case they're needed inside, and I should think the wagon has arrived from the morgue, along with members of the press, and believe me, ladies, I find the repetitive movements associated with murders most tiresome."

"Would it be more enjoyable if someone broke out in song and did a time step?" asked Bette.

Cayman laughed. And when his laughter subsided, he asked Agatha, "You seem a bit agitated, the way you're brutalizing your chin."

"I always rub it vigorously when something I'm after remains elusive."

"Such as?"

She squinted at the inspector and then got to her feet. "Here's a piece of information you need to know. When the Wynns moved out of here, they took their keys with them. Virgil urged them too. He wanted them to know that he still felt as though this was still their home."

"Quite nice of him," said the inspector.

Bette exploded. "Jesus! You mean they can invade this place anytime they feel like it? Why didn't Virgil tell me that? I'd have demanded they turn in their keys immediately. And I shall when they get here."

"You alerted them? How efficient."

"Agatha's the efficiency expert. I dread the possibility of getting an overdose of the Wynn family."

"I also called Nydia," said Agatha. "She also has a key."

"How very neat," said Cayman. "Here's a man who on the surface is portrayed as kind, generous, and thoughtful, and yet seems to have had a dark side that caused him to be murdered."

"There goes the door," said Bette.

"That would be the morgue. I'll have them wait in your reception room if you don't mind, Bette. I want to have a look downstairs before they remove Mamby."

"She has a sister," Agatha reminded him.

"She's not downstairs, is she?"

Agatha said patiently, "Inspector, you're very tired."

"As a matter of fact, I no longer am. Be back in half a mo'."

Bette refilled glasses. "He has a weird sense of humor. Do we wait for the inspector or shall we discuss who might have slain Mamby?"

"Oh, let's do be polite and wait for him."

"I wonder if any of the family are coming," said Bette.

"They're not needed. I did ask Nydia if she might come back."

"You didn't tell me you'd phoned her!"

"I thought she should know. She is involved."

"Was she shocked?"

"No." Agatha took her glass from Bette and sipped.

"You're not surprised."

"Nydia disliked Mamby. Nydia's the type who thinks servants should know their place and keep to it. To Nydia's taste, Mamby was too much a stereotype."

"Well, she was a bit of a one, wasn't she?"

"On the surface. With Mabel she was obsequious. With Roland she was brazenly rude. She mostly ignored Anthea and Oscar. She did her hardest work on Virgil. Good thing she's dead if she's not in the will. That might have killed her."

In the basement, Cayman stared at Mamby's corpse with undisguised distaste. He said to MacDougal, "You've removed the weapon."

MacDougal said jauntily. "It's done its job. Right smack into the aorta."

Cayman asked Nayland, who was poking about with a flashlight despite the overhead lighting, to get a better look at hidden recesses. "Any sign of a struggle?"

"None whatsoever. But there's the shovel and pick leaning upright against the stack of cartons. Mamby's ghost was prepared to continue his digging, apparently."

"She came down here to confront him," suggested Nayland.

156

"I suppose it would have to be a 'him.' No woman I can think of could handle that pick."

"I'll bet Mrs. Mallowan could. She's worked on expeditions with her husband."

Cayman smiled. He liked Agatha very much. "Perhaps she could. But she's an onlooker, not a participant. She murders only on paper. Mamby's ghost. I suppose she conjured up the ghost on her own." MacDougal was holding the weapon in a handkerchief. "Ambrose, how's for a butcher's?"

The coroner extended his hand. "Lovely object. Belongs in a museum, not in somebody's heart. The hilt's hand-carved. A very meticulous piece of artistry. I must say, they did have superior artisans back in those days, much better than what we've got around today."

"They didn't have hot and cold running water."

"Nayland," asked Cayman trying to sound subdued, "what in God's name does that have to do with this weapon?"

"Sorry. It just popped out. I spend a lot of time reading up on ancient civilizations. They were very colorful and very unsanitary. In those days, people rarely lived past forty."

"Thank you, Lloyd," said Cayman. "You have briefly broken the monotony of this investigation. Ambrose, turn the weapon in to the lab just for the hell it. I doubt if they'll learn anything, but at least we'll have gone through the motions. Find anything interesting, Lloyd? Footprints? Fingerprints?"

"Nothing fresh. A lot was erased by us when we came down earlier with the ladies. I'd like to make a suggestion."

"Go ahead. Delighted to accept all contributions."

"What about the pick and shovel? Oughtn't the lab to have a go at them?"

"A capital idea. Take them upstairs and give them to one of the boys. Ambrose, are you finished with Nellie?"

"Down here I am." He rubbed the palms of his hands together. "Now for the dissection."

"Tell me, Ambrose." He put an arm around the coroner's shoulders. "Don't you ever tire of autopsies?"

"Good heavens, no! I look upon each victim as a new adventure. No two corpses are alike."

"Really? Not even twins?"

"I've never done twins." He said with a faraway look in his eyes, "Perhaps someday."

Nayland, heading up the stairs with the pick and shovel, was stopped in mid-departure by Cayman. "I say, Lloyd. Send the boys down with the stretcher. There's not much more we can do down here." He stared down at Mamby. "Strange woman, this."

"More unfortunate than strange," said the coroner.

"I think we shall find, Ambrose darling, that the lady brought about her own misfortunes."

They were headed out of the basement. "A meddler, you think?" asked the coroner.

"Among other unpleasant attributes."

Nydia Tilson's high heels clickety-clacked as she half-walked, half-ran to Sloane Street, where she thought she'd have better luck finding a taxi. She had phoned several ranks after Agatha alerted her but none responded. She decided to brave her chances on the street. When she left her building, she could have sworn someone darted into the shadows of the adjoining alley. That frightened her. She thought of returning to her flat, but she was too anxious to get to the Wynn house. Nellie dead. Murdered. She rounded a corner upon hearing voices.

"There's safety in numbers."

She was in luck. The popular Jacaranda Club was still open. There were some taxis lined up waiting for future fares to exit the club. Nydia hurried towards the taxis, yoo-hooing and waving her hand. A taxi clattered away from the curb and picked her up. She gave the cabby the address and sank back with a sigh of relief. *Miss Bette Davis is certainly having a melodramatic initiation into* les affaires *Wynn. She'll hardly find her lawsuit as interesting. Smart lady. She got on to me quickly. Her suggestion I could be very successful in Holly-*

wood is tempting. There's a large British colony there, and I'm sure I could make inroads. There are several I know from my acting days. George Sanders. He's just getting started, but he'll do well. Brian Aherne. Heather Angel. Benita Hume. A lot of them. They could be useful.

The cabby was looking at her through his rearview mirror and thinking, I hope she's not going to be trouble, the way she's talking to herself and pounding the seat with her fists. We can't reach Blenheim Terrace too soon for me. On Abbey Road they passed, coming from the opposite direction, the ambulance transporting Nellie Mamby to the morgue. Had Nydia known Mamby was in the wagon, she might have saluted or, on a less flamboyant note, made a gentle gesture of farewell. Or perhaps, knowing her dislike of the woman, she might very probably have thumbed her nose.

In the Wynn drawing room, Bette was asking Cayman, "You mean the coroner has left without having even one drink? Why, Inspector, that's absolute cruelty. He's been at it all day long. Why, the poor thing. Has no one any consideration for him?"

Cayman explained with a twinkle, "Oh, Bette, poor Ambrose has a legion of the dead awaiting him in the morgue."

"Not really!"

"There are so many, the ice boxes are full and the rest are stacked from floor to ceiling. He's terribly understaffed and is beginning to wonder about enticing volunteers. Does that sort of thing interest you?"

"Now you're being funny, and that's just an expression, because you're not funny at all. Agatha, what's worrying you?"

"Mamby, in the basement."

"She's gone now." Bette stubbed a cigarette into a tray that cried to be emptied. At her suggestion, Nayland had a small blaze going in the fireplace to help ward off the chill.

"The body may be gone, but she's still very much present.

This morning she told us she thought the house was haunted and heard the digging in the basement and said nothing could get her down there to investigate. Why tonight?"

"Because like all the members of our cast of characters, Mamby was an outrageous liar." Cayman was standing with his hands clasped behind his back. A whisky Bette had poured for him when he and Nayland emerged from the basement with the coroner stood neglected on a nearby end table. Nayland, holding his glass, stood close to the fire, treasuring the warmth that flowed from it. Bette and Agatha shared the sofa but not their thoughts. Agatha's were with Mamby. Bette was contemplating the possibility of Nydia being the murderer, although how could she kill Mamby and be back in her flat on the other side of London in time to receive Agatha's call? She heard Cayman saying to her, "Don't you think they're all outrageous liars, Bette? I'm sure Mrs. Mallowan does."

Agatha rubbed her chin. "In all the years I've known the family, I've looked upon what you consider lies as sins of omission. Mabel was a great one for skipping over facts, and Lord knows Roland's long-winded sagas of his accomplishments carried a great deal of embroidery. As for Mamby, she never told a story the same way twice. I suppose, Inspector, we're both in mind of similar scenarios."

"I'll tell mine," said the inspector, "and along the way you can add or subtract when you feel the need to." He wondered if Bette ever ran out of cigarettes as she lit a new one. "I'm fairly sure Mamby was well aware of the identity of her ghost. I'm sure so was Virgil, and in his deteriorating state, he didn't much care. Mamby invented a ghost for our benefit. She didn't dare admit someone was down in the basement in the middle of the night hunting for buried treasure, or what I assume is buried treasure."

"Good heavens!" exclaimed Bette. "You don't suppose there could be a body!"

"If there were, I don't think anybody would be interested in exhuming it. No, it's more than likely there are valuables that Virgil hid away for safekeeping. He didn't care how much of the other stuff Mamby and his family pilfered. They're good pieces, but not top-notch. Am I correct, Mrs. Mallowan?"

"Of course you are. Why else would the government permit Virgil to store them on the premises? They fetch a price, but nothing like what are displayed in museums. In Egypt and Mesopotamia and all the other popular haunts of archeologists, artifacts are sold in shops catering to tourists and amateur collectors. I dread the thought of how many of King Tut's scepters are sold every year, and at varying prices, depending upon how astute the buyer is at haggling. It's a shame, but so much of it is a fraud."

Cayman drew their attention back to Nellie Mamby. "Tonight, I think Mamby had the courage of a lioness stalking her prey when she went down to the basement to confront the person she had referred to as a ghost."

"Blackmail," said Agatha.

"Indeed. Mamby had done her job and done it very well. Now that Virgil was dead and she knew the family were his heirs, she wanted more money than had been promised her."

Bette's eyes were about to pop. "Then it *was* she who was poisoning Virgil!"

"The same dose every day, disguised in sleeping draughts. Very carefully measured. Not too little."

"Yes," said Agatha. "Indeed yes. Otherwise, if she had given him too small doses daily, he would have built up a resistance to the poison and survived. The correct term for that, Bette, is 'mithridatism.'"

"Oh, God! Where do you find out these things?" Bette was impressed.

"Research, dear, research."

"How many books you must have read!"

"Of course," said Agatha, "to borrow from one book is plagiarism."

"To borrow from two books is research," completed Cayman. "Terribly old saw, that one."

"But still true," said Agatha with satisfaction.

"I thought Mamby was devoted to Virgil," said Bette.

"Inspector, may we digress for a moment while I explain something to Bette? To all three of you, as a matter of fact? Fine. Thank you. I think I'll stand. Now then, Mamby knew everything, or at least almost everything, that went on in this house. She was intimate with the family and with Mabel's friends at the salons, and let us not forget doctors and solicitors and tradesmen and the postman. Housekeepers seem to dote on postmen. I daresay Mamby had steaming open letters, especially official documents, and then resealing them down to a fine art. I should think she was almost as good at it as I used to be." She cleared her throat. "It led to problems with my first husband, which are of no importance here. Mamby therefore knew the contents of Virgil's will. Undoubtedly, she was thoroughly dissatisfied with what she'd been allotted. So she schemed to get more. The solution was quite simple. The others were nearly poverty-stricken and desperate for funds. Their future wealth was spelled out but, until Virgil died, unattainable. So Mamby went to work. She hinted to the others that Virgil had, in confidence, told her who was getting what."

Agatha interrupted, "I would think she began by preying on Anthea, she being the most desperate, what with those gambling debts. Then into her web she drew Oscar, he of the incredibly weak mind. And then she filled Sir Roland's head with the hope of reclaiming his glory if only he had the wherewithal to finance an expedition in search of Cleopatra's tomb. So Mamby became their ringleader."

Bette said, "I don't think she was capable of thinking up the poison plot."

"I agree," said Agatha. "Inspector, any ideas?"

"Three ideas, all Wynns, but how to prove it?"

162

Nayman broke his long silence. "Shouldn't you be considering Miss Tilson?"

"I don't know about anybody else, but I'm afraid I've been considering her all along. Except that she couldn't have killed Mamby and gotten to her home on the other side of town in time to receive Agatha's call.

"Nydia didn't kill Mamby," said Agatha. "One of the family did that. One who had access to arsenic or to someone who had access to arsenic."

Bette groaned. "I hate to think of Nydia as a murderer. She's been so kind to me."

"She had nothing to do with either death," Agatha stated flatly. "But she very obviously suspected the conspiracy. 'There's safety in numbers.' Frankly, my friends, I thought it was Nydia who'd be targeted as the next victim."

"There go the chimes. Nayland, would you do the honors?" Cayman said to Agatha and Bette, "Interesting that the family haven't arrived, either singly or en masse."

"Perhaps they're having a hasty meeting," suggested Bette. "Plotting strategy and all that. 'There's safety in numbers.'"

Agatha said, "I reached only Anthea and Oscar. Sir Roland was not at home, and I'm not yet prepared to make a conjecture."

11

"NAYLAND DELIVERED HIM TO HIS BLOCK of flats. Remember, he was in a peevish mood and slammed the car door shut and entered the building." Cayman cleared his throat. "Of course, it was a matter of perhaps a minute for Nayland to be out of sight and for Sir Roland to flag a cab. Perhaps he decided to go to the Explorers' Club for a nightcap."

Nydia Tilson came hurrying in, Nayland trailing behind her. "I had a terrible time getting a taxi. The cab ranks in my neighborhood are hopeless after midnight." She flung her coat onto a chair. "I had to go out into the street to find one and I had a terrible fright. I could have sworn there was someone lurking in the shadows of the alley next to my building."

"You're sure it wasn't your imagination?" asked Agatha. "Shadows of the night can play very strange tricks."

"Whatever it was, I ran like hell. Finally picked up a taxi outside the Jacaranda Club." She looked around the room. "Where's the family? Why aren't they here? Surely they were notified."

"Anthea and Oscar know. I couldn't rouse Roland," Agatha informed her. "They should be here, shouldn't they?

What with Virgil murdered this morning and now Mamby."

Bette contributed winsomely, "Perhaps they decided to skip it because there was no need to pay Mamby severance or whatever you call it in this country."

"We don't call it anything," said Cayman, "because we don't do it. In need of a drink, Mrs. Tilson? Bette pours with a delightfully free hand."

Bette defended herself. "We Americans are brought up to serve food in obscenely large portions and to serve very generous drinks. We're still recovering from Prohibition. Whisky, Nydia?"

"Any port in a storm. Whisky's fine. Thank God the fog's let up, or I'd have been truly frantic out there." She was lighting a cigarette. "I suppose, Inspector, Mamby's murder plays hob with your schedule of interviews for tomorrow."

He ignored her remark or seemed to. "Bette, have you been inside Mamby's room?"

"Rooms, plural. Yes, when Virgil took me on a tour of the house the first time Nydia brought me here. Nydia accompanied us on the tour. I was rather surprised by the size of Mamby's quarters. It's more like a suite of rooms in a hotel. There's a sitting room, bedroom, and bath."

"And artifacts," added Nydia. "A very impressive display of them. I remember commenting on them, and Mamby didn't bat an eyelash. You were a bit surprised too, weren't you, Bette?"

"Well, frankly, I sort of thought they were appropriate decor. I mean the bloody things are all over the place. I could never begin to decide their value."

Agatha said, "They'll need to be catalogued. Everything in the place. As I recall, ladies, I asked you last night to start cataloguing them this morning."

Bette reminded her, "There were matters that caused us to postpone it."

"Mrs. Tilson, now that you're here, do you mind if I take

the time to ask a few questions? In fact, it might make your appearance at the Yard tomorrow unnecessary," said Cayman.

Agatha asked reluctantly, "Would you like Bette and me to leave?"

"I very much want you to stay. You're both superb sounding boards."

Bette was heard muttering, "Sounding board. That's a new one on me. I've been called all sorts of things, but never a sounding board."

"Don't be obtuse, dear," cautioned Agatha. "He simply appreciates our sticking our oars in. Most investigators don't. Egos bruise so easily in the police department. Every man a Sherlock Holmes, you know."

"Nydia, do you object to our presence?" Bette asked politely, promising herself that she'd strangle Nydia if her friend protested hers and Agatha's presence.

"Of course not. As a matter of fact, I feel much more comfortable with the two of you and your moral support."

"And 'there's safety in numbers,' " said Cayman, terribly pleased with himself.

"I suppose I'll never live that down," said Nydia.

Cayman asked, "Was that an improvisation or part of your original scenario?"

Nydia sat up. "All séances are improvised. We mediums take our cues from the departed we manage to contact."

"Mrs. Tilson. Please, dear Mrs. Tilson. You knew exactly what you wished to accomplish with the séance."

"And I did. I spoke to Virgil."

Cayman said with exaggerated patience, "I never met Virgil Wynn, so I can't attest to the authenticity of his voice. But Mrs. Mallowan complimented you by saying it was a pretty good piece of mimicry."

"Virgil whispered," Agatha reminded Nydia.

"Possibly a touch of laryngitis," defended Nydia.

"Now, really, Nydia," said Bette.

"Mrs. Tilson," said Cayman, towering over her, "you were using the séance to cast suspicion of the attempted murder of Virgil Wynn on the other three surviving members of his family and Nellie Mamby."

If Nydia had any composure to lose, it never started slipping away. Bette found herself admiring the woman's defiance of Cayman's accusation.

"Exactly how am I to interpret your statement?" asked Nydia.

"You suspected the three Wynns and Mamby were in a conspiracy to systematically poison Virgil. I rather think it's been your suspicion for quite a while. Virgil's stabbing made you come to the decision to try and bring the plot to a boil. So, rather than go to Scotland Yard with your suspicion, you chose a more familiar route, a séance."

"Inspector, would Scotland Yard have believed me? Would *you* have believed me?"

"Possibly."

"Codswallop!" she snapped. "You're quite right. I've suspected for months they were killing Virgil. I discussed it with Virgil. I discussed it with his doctor, Solomon Hubbard, but that doddering old duffer said I had an overactive imagination. He was positive Virgil was the victim of some wasting disease that was rife in parts of North Africa. And for a while I thought perhaps he was right. So did Virgil. Virgil's days fluctuated. There were good days and there were bad days. But the bad days began to outnumber the good ones, and I began to suspect something truly was afoot. I read up on poisons. Remember, Agatha? You were kind enough to let me use your private library."

"I'm very generous that way," said Agatha, "even when some people dog-ear the pages."

Cayman asked, "Why didn't you confront any of the family with your suspicion?"

"And become a marked woman? I had no proof. Even now there's no proof." She was warming up. "Why was Virgil stabbed, when the killer must have known his death was imminent? Why was Mamby murdered?"

"Virgil Wynn was murdered in a fit of uncontrollable anger," said Cayman, very much in control. "Virgil came back here last night for a prearranged meeting with his killer. It was something, I suspect, to do with the notes Virgil presumably had forgotten to take with him earlier that evening. If these notes exist, I suspect they confirmed his suspicion of how he was being murdered and by whom. At one point Virgil said something that infuriated his murderer, and as Virgil threw back his head with his mouth open in a burst of mocking laughter, the killer picked up the weapon from the desk and plunged it into his throat."

He paused to let his statements sink in. When he continued, his voice was subdued. "Virgil knew that if he was truly being poisoned, the tool was Nellie Mamby. She had complete access to his medicines. She could doctor them. She prepared his meals, albeit you and the rest, contributing occasional dishes, might also have been responsible, save for the fact that a precise dose of arsenic had to be administered. Too much would have killed him at once, and that wasn't wanted. That would have meant an immediate suspicion of murder and a thorough investigation. Too little and he'd have been building up an immunity to the poison." He paused for a moment to arrange his thoughts. "As to Nellie Mamby, Agatha has explained that she took to steaming open Virgil's mail and therefore was privy to his private papers. She didn't like her position in his will and wanted more, so she decided to blackmail for it. By the way, she was murdered with the same weapon." Nydia gasped. "After Virgil's death, the murderer brought the weapon to the basement, cleaned it of blood and fingerprints, and hid it in a safe place, probably not sure it would come in handy again. Virgil's murder was premeditated by the group. Nellie Mamby's murder was premeditated by one person acting alone."

Nydia said shrilly, "I was not a conspirator in Virgil's murder and I most certainly did not murder Nellie, though there have been times in the past when I would have been delighted to do so."

"Mrs. Tilson, there's a misunderstanding here. I have not accused you of anything other than being remiss in not bringing your suspicion to the police." She moved to remonstrate, and Tilson held up a hand to stop her. "I know. I know. You feared your suspicion would have been doubted and you'd have been made to appear a fool."

Agatha spoke up. "Inspector, I more than see Nydia's point and I respect it. I think she did a good enough job with the séance, though I could have done without the French actress and Mabel."

"I'm terribly sorry, Agatha," said Nydia indignantly, "but there had to be a build-up to Virgil."

"Of course," agreed Bette. "You can never start the show with the star turn, you have to do a warm-up with the jugglers and the trained seals. Right, Nydia? I did adore Joan of Arc."

"Yes," agreed Agatha. "Nicely done. Why didn't you bring in Ogden?"

"What?" Nydia's voice drooped in pain.

"Your late husband. Ogden. Have you forgotten him so soon? It would have been a charming touch to know that they're all having a reunion off somewhere on an astral plane where spectral get-togethers are much the thing. And I remember Ogden being terribly fond of Virgil and his mother. What I've been wondering lately is, exactly how really fond of Mabel was Virgil?"

"Too fond," said Nydia, her voice frigid. "Hamlet and Queen Gertrude."

"I'm *dying* to play Ophelia," said Bette, wondering why they were all giving her strange looks. She decided she wasn't being fast enough with the booze and set to work remedying what she thought was the situation. She couldn't wait to phone her mother in Los Angeles and tell her the latest, which her mother would surely make capital of at her next bridge game.

Nydia directed a question to Bette. "Didn't you hear the murderer come into the house?"

"No," said Bette, "but I heard him go."

Agatha told Nydia, "Bette is aware that the family and you have keys to the house, as does the inspector. Mr. Nayland, I wonder, could I trouble you to place another log on the fire? It's terribly chilly in here. Bette, have you a fire going upstairs?"

"I'm not bothered by the cold. We Yankees—"

"Please, Bette," Agatha interrupted her. "I know all about you Yankees. Isn't there a baseball team with that name?"

"Yes, there is, Agatha. But they are ball players, and we are a state of mind." She added swiftly, "I would have liked to hear Ogden. He sounds such a nice chap."

"He was," said Agatha. "Nydia, did he and Virgil really like each other?"

"What's that got to do with the present unpleasantness?"

"Frankly, my dear, I really don't know. But my subconscious does strange things from time to time, and now it's at work again and up pops Ogden."

Bette suggested, "Perhaps he'll soon pop back again."

"Perhaps we ought to stop popping and get back to cases," suggested Cayman, fighting hard to keep his temper in check. And what the hell is Mrs. Mallowan up to, he wondered, considering taking her by the arm, ushering her into the library, and asking her point blank what she thought Mrs. Tilson's late husband had to do with the case.

"I'd like to answer, Agatha," said Nydia. "Ogden and Virgil were very good friends. You know that Ogden was one of Virgil's backers."

"Shame on me!" cried Agatha, sounding like Alice's Red Queen demanding that heads be removed. "How could I have forgotten that?"

Quite conveniently, thought Bette, but didn't say so. Sly puss, thought Bette. Agatha's working on something and she'll soon spring it on us, and I'll bet it's a lulu. She caught Cayman's eye briefly. His returned to Nydia.

"Mrs. Tilson," asked Cayman, "you firmly believe in your . . . um . . . gift, don't you?"

"If I didn't, it wouldn't work."

"So we're to believe you were really in contact with Virgil and Mabel?"

Nydia was on her feet and pacing back and forth. "Inspector, I told you earlier that at the séance to try and contact Houdini I had what one might call a visitation. I didn't recognize it. It was pointed out to me. I realized then that it was not the first time this had happened to me. I wondered if perhaps my mind was failing, but an alienist I consulted assured me that was not the case. I asked him if he could interpret these visitations, and he told me about studies that were being made in extrasensory perception and out-of-body experiences. The studies are terribly primitive and I was invited to join an experimental group." She took a dramatic pause, being the fine actress she was. "I astonished them. If you like, I'll identify the group and give them permission to discuss my gift with you."

"I trust your information," said Cayman, and Bette liked him even more.

"I underwent hypnosis several times, and they later told me I had spoken in a variety of voices on each occasion and that I had identified most of the voices. Among the voices I identified was my maternal grandmother; also Mrs. Siddons, the actress, who said she was my guardian angel, and I happily believed her; one of the Borgia women, and I spoke in Italian, a language of which I know nothing except 'Ciao' and various forms of pasta. What I'm trying to explain is that I am not in control of my gift; it controls me. Which is why I have to be very careful. I sometimes black out. Very annoying."

Bette said, "I think you blacked out tonight. Your head fell forward. You were very still. It worried me."

"The truth is, I black out when I feel I'm getting out of control. I know I came through as Mabel, screeching, but whatever it is I said in her voice, it had to be her, as I never knew Mabel to scream, screech, yell, or whatever. I never witnessed any fit of anger of Mabel's I tell you, what I said tonight had to be authentic!"

"I agree," said Sir Roland, entering the room on little cat feet. "Forgive me, Bette. I let myself in."

"To pay me a visit? And at this hour?"

"Actually, no. I happened to phone Oscar, and he told me he'd heard from Agatha that Mamby had been stabbed to death, and I assumed we were all wanted here. So I let myself in with my key. It's deuced cold out there and I was too impatient to wait for someone to answer the door."

"What with Mamby dead and inoperable," said Bette. "Mr. Nayland, would you pour a drink for Sir Roland?" She said to Sir Roland, "I'm sure you can use one."

Sir Roland dropped his coat and hat on Nydia's coat. He didn't answer Bette. Sir Roland said to Cayman, "I gather you're questioning the authenticity of Nydia as a medium." Cayman said nothing. "That was Mabel indeed, and at her most vicious. Forgive me, Nydia. Virgil was passable, though some of your embellishments were a bit too much, but should you survive me, I'd be delighted to receive you should you consider trying to contact me."

Cayman asked Sir Roland, "Are your son and daughter coming?"

"Oscar is with Anthea at her flat. After Agatha phoned her with the unpleasant news, Anthea phoned Oscar in the midst of rising hysteria, which then erupted into a case of complete hysteria, and so Oscar went to be with her after I spoke to him." He paused to take a glass of whisky from Nayland. Referring to the whisky, Sir Roland asked, "Wasn't it Bernard Shaw who referred to this as mother's milk?"

"It was gin he was referring to," said Agatha. "Spoken by Eliza in *Pygmalion*."

"Sir Roland, I must tell you that it is suspected your son's murder was the result of a conspiracy to kill him."

Sir Roland's hand holding the glass halted midway on its way to his mouth. "You mean a group held the instrument that stabbed him?"

"No, that was the work of one person. The group conspired to slowly poison your son to death."

"Well. Well. Well. And this group? Of whom does it consist?"

"Your son Oscar; your daughter, Anthea; Nellie Mamby; and yourself."

"Do you have proof of this preposterous accusation?"

Strange, thought Bette. He isn't storming, he isn't raging, he hasn't flung the glass of whisky at Cayman. Of course, he's very wisely underplaying.

"I intend to have it after I have interrogated all of you seperately, if not sooner."

"Inspector, you haven't been listening," said Agatha with an intensity that annoyed Cayman.

"Listening to what?" he snapped.

"You have forgotten what Bette told us about the importance of listening. What Ethel Barrymore taught her."

"Oh, I never said I'd met Ethel Barrymore. I said I'd learned from watching her. So you see, Agatha, you haven't listened all that carefully either."

Still unnerved by Cayman's rough interrogation, Nydia was wondering if everyone in the room would understand if she decided to have a nervous breakdown. Nayland's eyes were on Sir Roland, whose glass-holding hand seemed to be paralyzed in midair. Agatha maintained a questioning look directed at Cayman, while Cayman returned her gaze, his face slowly reddening, now realizing he had missed something important in his anxiety to try and catch Sir Roland off guard.

But it was Agatha who had caught Sir Roland off guard.

"Inspector, don't look so bemused. You've had a maddening time of it. I don't blame you for not hearing words which when I repeat them, you will realize at great delight are incriminating."

Sir Roland at last relaxed his hand, but he sipped none of the whisky. Agatha had him in her spotlight.

Agatha spoke slowly and succinctly. "You said, Roland, 'I happened to phone Oscar, and he told me he'd heard from Agatha that Mamby had been stabbed to death.'" She paused, and her eyes returned to Cayman. "I never told Oscar any such thing, nor did I say that to Anthea when I rang her. I never mentioned how Mamby had been killed. I merely said she'd been found murdered in the basement." She took a breath, and her eyes were focused again on Sir Roland. "Roland, I daresay we needn't conjecture as to how you knew Mamby had been stabbed to death."

12

OUTSIDE THE WYNN HOUSE SEVERAL NEWSPAPER REPORTERS
and photographers were milling about in the raw night air,
exhaling steam as they spoke and not being too kind about the
facts being withheld from them. The detectives guarding the
door had let Sir Roland enter with his key, having recognized
him from earlier in the day. What little they knew they'd
heard from the morgue attendants who carried the body from
the house. They knew the housekeeper had been murdered
and shared the information with the press, who considered
the brief news the equivalent of a starvation diet. One photog-
rapher made his way to the side of the house, intending to
climb over the brick wall, but was quickly collared by one of
Cayman's more astute men. Lights were on in the houses that
faced those of Virgil Wynn and Agatha Christie, and every so
often a face appeared in a window, piqued by curiosity, wondering what was going on.

They'd read all about Virgil in the evening papers and either
felt sorry for him or felt that it served him right. There was no
middle ground of opinion, as there was no basis for it. Virgil
had not been terribly outgoing or even slightly friendly with
his neighbors. A few veterans of the cul-de-sac reminisced
about the good old days of Mabel's salons and the expensive

automobiles depositing expensively dressed celebrities at the Wynn door.

Inside the house, in the drawing room, Bette was all silent admiration for Agatha Mallowan. She felt sorry for Cayman because Agatha had put one over on him, but Agatha wasn't gloating, and Bette felt pleased that her dissertation on listening had unmasked a murderer. Sir Roland now sat near the fire, hunched over his glass of whisky and speaking very huskily. Bette didn't know why she felt sorry for him, but she did.

Sir Roland was speaking. His voice was so soft, Bette had to strain to understand him. "You don't know what it's like to fall from the height of fame and fortune to a grim cellar of despair. To attribute this despairing fate to members of your family. Your son, your wife. To learn that these people you loved and esteemed were perverse monsters." He lifted his head and Bette saw his eyes were moist. "I'm a very proud man, Inspector. And I have found out that pride truly goeth before a fall. I was on top of the world when I discovered Queen Baramar's tomb. I was in headlines. I was in newsreels. I earned tons of money, which meant that at last I could assert my position as the head of my household, no longer dependent on my wife's money to sustain us. Mabel seemed to be so proud of me."

Now his eyes seemed afire. "Can you imagine how I felt when I returned to England, acclaimed an international hero? It was the kind of glory I should have known I'd never again experience. But I was blinded by success, intoxicated with it, reveling in it. I thought it would go on forever."

"Poor Roland," said a sympathetic Agatha. "Nothing goes on forever."

He contradicted her. "Mabel went on forever. Mabel blossomed. She husbanded her assets and went to work on mine. It was a Mabel I had never known. Not the woman I had fallen in love with and courted and won against a great deal of competition. It seemed every desirable bachelor was pursuing her, unlike what you said in the séance, Nydia."

"It was Mabel," said Nydia. "You yourself agreed."

"It was a side of Mabel I thought only I had experienced. The shrew, the bitch. That nonsense about wanting to lose her virginity. She had long since traded that in for a mess of pottage. A Romanov prince who threw her over for a contortionist in a Continental circus. Mabel married me on the rebound. She was right. I was available. Very available. I was besotted with her." He paused. "No, in truth, I was besotted with her wealth. The wealth I needed to outfit my expedition in search of Baramar. Agatha, did you know I asked Max to be my partner?"

"Yes, I did know. Max will be forever grateful. But Max is a lone wolf. He prefers to work alone."

"He told me to be the same. He helped with my financing." He stared at the fire. "Not a bloody penny from Mabel."

Bette wondered if, in his mind, he was watching Mabel going up in flames. For his peace of mind, she hoped it was slow and with much suffering.

Sir Roland continued, "Nydia, it was Ogden who completed my financing."

"So he told me," said Nydia.

"I'm happy he realized a good profit. I thought I was profiting too. Commercial endorsements. Speaking engagements. Articles for magazines and newspapers. It came rolling in like a Niagara. And Mabel spent and spent. We bought this house, and I little suspected the conspiracy between Virgil, Mabel, and Ogden Tilson."

All eyes were on Nydia. Her face betrayed nothing.

Sir Roland continued, "Mabel wanted Virgil to be a great archeologist too. Virgil was an all too willing disciple. Thanks to me, he developed a great fascination with the ancient worlds of Egypt and Mesopotamia. I thought he took such great pride in my accomplishments. But Mabel had poisoned his mind against me. Mabel never loved me, I realized. Women rarely love the men they marry on the rebound, or so I've heard."

"Not all women," said Agatha. "I married Max on the rebound and we've been bouncing merrily ever since."

Bette wondered if 'bouncing' was quite the word Agatha had really intended to use. It was difficult to conjure up a vision of Agatha bouncing with anyone. As far as Bette was concerned, Agatha Mallowan was definitely not the bouncing type.

"As my fortunes descended, Virgil's rose. Howard Carter and Lord Carnarvon had already confirmed my unfortunate lot when they found King Tut's tomb. And now Howard and I commiserate with each other, bemoan our fate, never daring to admit we should have fought harder and dirtier, the way Virgil and other of his contemporaries did and still do. Virgil's uncovering of the first Ptolemy, I must admit, was spectacular. Films, motion pictures, that is, now had a primitive form of color, two-strip, I believe it was called, and Ptolemy's tomb indeed made a fabulous series of color photographs. He was a hero. Myself, Howard Carter, some other tragic figures, we were dodoes. Extinct. Looked back upon with curiosity. He and his mother had me in their clutches. I was broke. I was dependent on Mabel again. She made me a small allowance, as did Virgil. They did the same for Anthea and Oscar, who have problems."

Oh, brother! confirmed Bette. The look on Agatha's face warned Bette to withold any comment or be struck down by Agatha's bolt of lightning.

"Anthea and Oscar are not stable people. Oscar buries himself in his music, Anthea in her poetry. They were never encouraged by either me or Mabel. We were too selfishly involved in our own concerns. It wasn't until recently that we found any kind of rapport with each other." He chuckled, dry and lifeless. "It was Virgil who brought about the rapport. Ironic, don't you think?"

"Rather tragic," said Bette, happy to hear her own voice again.

"It wasn't too difficult drawing Mamby into our conspiracy," said Sir Roland. "That woman was one of the nastiest pieces I have ever encountered."

"Why didn't you get rid of her?" asked Agatha.

Sir Roland exploded. "I finally did, didn't I?" He held out his empty glass. "Anybody. The sanctuary that only whisky can afford a tired, old, old man." Nayland took his glass for the refill.

Bathos, thought Bette. How I loathe bathos. A tired old man my foot. First he digs up coffins and then reverses the procedure and helps to fill them. She wondered who could play him in the movie. Of course. Henry Stephenson! Perfect. He's always busy. If he's not available we fall back on old reliable C. Aubrey Smith.

Cayman was asking Sir Roland a question. "When did you four conspire to kill Virgil?"

"Shortly after Mabel's will was read, leaving him the giant share of her fortune and leaving us small trusts from which we could draw only so much yearly. It was unfair, and it wasn't too hard to convince Anthea and Oscar to agree with me. On top of this, Virgil announced he was planning to sell the house and construct a museum in his own honor, to which would be attached living quarters for himself."

"Did you know about this, Mrs. Tilson?" asked Cayman.

"Yes. Ogden told me."

"Did you discuss it with Virgil?"

"Why should I have? It was Virgil's business. Virgil's money. It had nothing to do with me. But I don't think he really intended to sell this house. I think it was a hint to his family that he preferred they live elsewhere."

"And yet he told them to keep their keys to this house," said Cayman. Nydia shrugged.

Bette said, "Keys can be copied, can't they?" Agatha nodded in tacit agreement. "Maybe Virgil didn't know they had the keys copied. Sir Roland, did you three copy your keys?"

"Guilty as charged," said Sir Roland solemnly. "But in time, Virgil guessed what we had done. We three systematically pilfered from the basement. Oh, I know what you're thinking. This once-honorable man had taken to stealing from his son's basement." He smiled. "It had to be from the basement, because that's where the stuff was stored."

"Say, wait a minute!" cried Bette as she ignited a cigarette. "What's buried in the grave?"

"That's what I've been trying to find out these tiring nights," admitted Sir Roland. "I suspect it's various articles that I brought back from Baramar's tomb. They disappeared while I was away on a speaking tour. It wasn't until recently that I wondered if they might not ever have left the premises. Possibly buried in the garden. Then it occurred to me that the garden could be too dicey, especially with Agatha's house overlooking it." He smiled at Agatha. "And we all know Agatha has terribly sharp eyes."

"And terribly sharp ears," added Bette with a loving smile.

"It had to be the basement," concluded Sir Roland, "and by God I was right. I tested the floor several times till I found the area where I suspected the grave was hidden. I think I'm right. If you continue digging, Inspector, I think you will truly find buried treasure."

"So you were Mamby's ghost," said Agatha.

"A little *divertissement* on her part to warn me she'd give the game away if I didn't increase her share. Well, there's no need for that now."

"Tell me about last night." Nayland stared at Cayman as he spoke. Nayland also marveled at how Sir Roland's refill was so quickly in need of a refill. Bette was amazed at her own capacity for this whisky, until she later learned that spirits sold in Great Britain had a much smaller alcoholic proof than those sold abroad.

"What about last night?"

"Your farewell dinner with Virgil. When he left to return here to look for notes he presumably forgot to take with him when he moved to his club."

"Inspector, am I now accused of having stabbed Virgil in the throat?"

"Sir Roland, you wouldn't want the credit to go elsewhere."

Sir Roland now looked and sounded like a pixie. "I *have* been rather busy lately, haven't I? Such energy from a retired has-been."

"Oh, don't say that word," cried Bette.

"Why shouldn't he?" asked Agatha. "Is there another of those ridiculous theatrical superstitions attached to it?"

"No. But it's a cruel word. There should be no such expression in anyone's vocabulary. Once-well-known players, former stars, are now forced to play small parts, walk-ons, more or less, or work as extras in order to survive. I hate it when I'm told that a crowd scene is populated by a host of has-beens. I find myself looking about, subtly, I hope, to figure out which these people are. Then I have this recurring nightmare that someday they'll be pointing at an actress and saying she's a has-been and the actress they'll be pointing at will be *me!*"

"Well, Bette, darling," said Agatha in the face of Bette's alarm over the possible tragic fate that might be awaiting her, "you must invest your money wisely!"

"If I can ever get my hands on any!"

"Ladies, ladies," said Cayman with exaggerated patience. The ladies retreated into silence. "Sir Roland, about stabbing Virgil."

"At dinner, he revealed that he knew I was digging in the basement. He also said he was going back to the house to draw up notes for his solicitor that would reveal he knew of the conspiracy to poison him and hence nullify and void his will. He spewed such venom. I followed him back to the house. Mamby knew we were there. She'd been in the kitchen and first heard Virgil arrive, followed by me shortly after. Virgil shut the drawing-room door after I arrived so that Bette wouldn't hear us. He knew he was too far gone to make it to Egypt. But it wasn't too late for him to set things right. Ladies and gentlemen, let me elucidate a point concerning Virgil. He wasn't the brightest person in the world. He was in fact as dense as his siblings. He didn't want to believe he was being poisoned. He wanted to believe what the doctor had told him. He was dying of some exotic disease playing havoc throughout North Africa. But he finally had the sense to go to the British Museum and consult a book on poisons."

"He could have troubled me," said Agatha, "although the traffic in my library was a bit heavy at times."

"Arsenic seemed to tally with his symptoms. Fainting spells, loss of appetite, discoloration of the fingernails, loss of hair. Poor sod. When Mabel was alive, he gardened with her almost daily. Couldn't he remember she had a reserve of arsenic in the potting shed for killing weeds?"

"This is all so cold-blooded," whispered Bette.

"Even for a Yankee?" asked Agatha.

Sir Roland's speech gained momentum. "He asked, 'Who's poisoning me? Who's doing this to me?' And I said, 'Why don't you go to hospital and save yourself?' But he said he knew he was too far gone. He'd barely made it to the dinner. It was a Herculean effort to get himself back here. But then he began saying terrible things about me. And terrible things Mabel had said about me. That I was a fraud! I deserved no honors, I didn't deserve to be knighted, she knew that others on my expedition had actually discovered the tomb while I was in a neighboring village fornicating with a Muslim prostitute! Then he threw back his head and laughed that openmouthed, obscene laugh of his, and I picked up the instrument from the desk and in a white-hot rage plunged it into his mouth." He paused. "You can imagine the look of astonishment on his face. You might also imagine the look of astonishment on mine. When I removed the weapon, he began gurgling. I didn't want him spewing blood all over that lovely desk. I clamped his mouth shut in the midst of his death rattle. I wrapped the knife in a handkerchief, extinguished the light, and carried the weapon to the basement, where I cleaned it and placed it on a carton next to the grave."

"Where you had occasion to use it on Mamby tonight."

"Yes."

"Really, Roland," said Agatha in exasperation. "How could you have been silly enough to try digging tonight when you should have been at home in mourning for your son, which would have been very hypocritical of you—"

"But it would have made a hell of a lot more sense!" said Bette.

"I lay my stupidity at the feet of greed. But oh, oh, oh, the awful things he was saying!" He stared at Nydia. "You knew, didn't you?"

"Knew what? What are you talking about?"

"The viciousness with which you portrayed Mabel at the séance."

"It *was* Mabel. I insist it was!" Her eyes implored Agatha for help, but Agatha chose to stay neutral.

Sir Roland leapt to his feet, fists clenched, raging uncontrollably, his face so red that Bette feared he'd have an apoplectic fit. "You knew that Mabel and Ogden were having an affair!"

"Liar!" snarled Nydia, and it looked terribly unbecoming. "You liar!"

"They were having an affair! You knew, but you never told me! I had to come upon them unexpectedly in a disgusting display of animal passion out in the garden, in the gazebo."

Bette stared at Agatha. "Animal passion in a gazebo? It's unheard-of!"

"You're hearing it now," said Agatha coolly, and loving every bit of this display of outraged anger.

"Ogden loved me! He loved me, I say! He left me his fortune!"

Agatha continued coolly, "Well, it's the decent thing to do. There's got to be some compensation for a husband's caddish behavior."

Nydia wheeled on Agatha. "Are you saying this is true?" Agatha's face was as blank as Anthea's verse. "You knew about the affair?"

"My dear Nydia, I understand your shock and why you're carrying on, but I simply don't understand why you didn't suspect them."

"Why should I have?"

"Because Ogden was spending more time in this house than he was spending with you."

"I thought he was here spending time with Virgil! Planning their next expedition!"

"Dear Nydia," said Agatha as Bette brought her a new glass of whisky, "there was definitely a dig under discussion around here, but it was the one shared by Mabel and Ogden. Please! Don't hate me! Max wanted me to tell you, but I refused to get involved. I have enough of my own problems."

"Oh, Agatha," said Bette, "now you sound like Jack Warner. Hmmmm . . . arsenic . . . slow poisoning . . ."

Nydia said archly, which made Bette wonder if Agatha had been a good judge of Nydia's performance in the Wilde play, "You let me live in a fool's paradise."

"I let you do nothing of the sort," said Agatha. "Frankly, I thought you did know and didn't give a damn. You were up there in your own special pantheon, thanks to your remarkable success as a medium, and there was Ogden's wealth to consider."

"Wealth isn't everything!" stormed Nydia.

"Oh no?" Bette exhaled ferociously.

"Well, Inspector, you're certainly getting an unexpected earful," said Agatha. "Well, why not? You're a hardworking man and you deserve a bonus." She spoke to Nydia. "Had I grassed to you about Mabel and Ogden, what would you have done about it? I suppose you'd have confronted Ogden in a facsimile of one of those scenes Frederick Lonsdale used to write so cleverly. Ogden, flustered, would have flub-dubbed all over the place. If you'd asked for a divorce he would probably been frantic to try and change your mind, because, Nydia, I absolutely believe you are the only woman other than perhaps his nanny whom Ogden really loved.''

Nydia was standing and drew herself up with fingers interlaced. Bette was thinking she'd certainly play this scene differently, especially if she were up against a scene stealer like May Robson or Lucile Watson. Nydia said, "If Ogden had really loved me, he would never have cheated.''

"Oh, no? Christie said he loved me, but how he cheated! There are so many married men to whom cheating comes as a second nature!''

Bette wondered about Ham. Had he cheated on her? Who with? Anyone she knew? And why did she care? She no longer loved him.

"Why, Bette, my dear, you're blushing!'' said a wide-eyed Agatha.

"I suppose I am. Am I really?''

"I do believe that beneath that Yankee exterior there lies a prude! I thought you Hollywood ladies were the prototypes of the worldly.''

"I was thinking about cheating.''

"Now, that's truly worldly. With whom?''

"Agatha, you're a bit confused.'' Cayman was a bit interested. If Bette Davis was thinking of cheating, he hoped he led her list. "I was thinking about my husband asking me if I'd been to bed with one of my co-stars.''

"I'm thirsting to hear your reply.''

"I didn't reply because I've not been to bed with him, but I'm thirsting to, as you so quaintly put it, and I shall assuage that thirst as soon as I get back to Hollywood.''

"Such self-confidence. Are you sure he'll be available?''

"Very sure. Very available. Cigarette, Nydia?''

Cayman saw an opening and grabbed it. "Ladies, if we may get back to the subject of murder and''—he couldn't resist—"our very versatile Sir Roland Wynn.'' Bette and Nydia were lighting up, while Bette was toying with an idea she was afraid might backfire. "Sir Roland, I will charge you with the murder of Nellie Mamby. As to Virgil's murder, I shall have a bit of sorting-out to do there. The poisoning was a conspiracy of four, but the knife in Virgil's throat was strictly your own doing."

"Sort of the icing on the cake," said Bette with a small smile. She was thinking, In for a penny, in for a pound. "Inspector, I think there's another loose end that needs tying up."

"Yes?"

"The possibility that Mabel Wynn was murdered." She was looking at Nydia as she spoke. Nydia was staring at the smoking tip of her cigarette. Agatha wore a half-smile, admiring Bette for saying what was also on Agatha's mind.

"And what leads you to believe Lady Wynn did not commit suicide, as is officially listed?"

"Inspector, I'm a very quick study. I can learn scenes by just scanning the pages. And as I'm sure by now you're very tired of hearing, I'm a very good listener. Mabel, if it was Mabel—"

"It *was* Mabel." Agatha expected to see icicles forming on Nydia's mouth.

"All right. It was Mabel. And quite articulate too. Stop staring at me like that, Nydia, you're making me uncomfortable and you've no cause to." She stared at the ceiling. "Now, let me be sure I've got it right." She was on her feet, standing in the center of the room, smoking cigarette held between the index and middle fingers of her right hand. And then she did an almost perfect imitation of Mabel's voice as she heard it at the séance. " '*It wasn't at all bitter. It was so easy to drink. I wasn't at all afraid. I was so sure I'd be afraid of Death.*' " She waited for a comment from Cayman.

"That was superb," marveled Agatha. "You have a wonderful ear for voices. Wasn't that superb, Roland? Didn't it make you feel Mabel was right here in the room with us?"

"She could very well be," said Nydia.

Agatha consulted her wristwatch. "I think not. It's a bit late for Mabel. She's probably tucked away in bed by now. Well, Bette? What do you suppose wasn't at all bitter and so easy to drink?"

"Arsenic. I think that's what killed her. Not an overdose of a sleeping draught, though it's probable it was a sleeping draught laced with a fatal dose of arsenic."

Sir Roland's voice intervened. It was tired and hoarse and not his normal voice at all. "I swear it, and I'll swear it on a stack of Bibles. I did not murder my wife."

"I didn't say you did. I simply said I thought she was murdered."

Sir Roland leaned forward. For a moment Bette was afraid he'd lose his balance and fall face first to the floor. "She was in agony. Drugs were no longer useful. She pleaded for mercy. But I swear by all that's holy I didn't prepare the fatal potion." He spat the next sentence. "I no longer loved her." He continued viciously, "She loathed me. She ruined me. She was as nasty as she emerged in the séance. Nastier!" He smiled and there was mockery in it. "I wanted her to go on suffering forever. I loved hearing her pleading with God to take her. But her God was also my God, and I prefer to think he favored me over her and to please me kept her alive so I could watch and hear her suffering."

"There, there, old boy," soothed Cayman. "Calm yourself." He said to Bete, "The words 'it wasn't at all bitter' could easily pertain to a drink other than poison."

"Like most of us, I'm sure Mabel thought all poisons had horrible tastes. Perhaps she didn't know arsenic has no taste. Isn't that so, Agatha? You're my source of information." Bette's eyes sparkled.

"Absolutely tasteless."

"There. You see?"

"See what?" asked Cayman.

"See that she didn't realize she was being murdered. She probably thought she was being given a triple or quadruple serving of her sleeping draught. Well, I know enough about that stuff to tell you you must take a precise amount or else all you'll do is make yourself horribly ill, upchucking all over the place."

Agatha said with a look of undisguised distaste, " 'Up-chucking'! What a revolting word!"

"Not nearly as revolting as 'has-been'!" Bette shot back.

With arms folded, the very tired inspector asked Bette, "And who do you suppose fed Lady Wynn the poison?"

"The only person in the world she truly trusted."

Nydia shouted, "Not Ogden! Never Ogden!"

Annoyed, Bette said, "My dear Nydia. Ogden was her lover. You never trust a lover." She took a long drag on her cigarette and then, looking at Sir Roland, said pointedly and with the sort of fervor that was becoming an acting trademark, "Quite obviously—that is, to me, and I think to Agatha—Mabel Wynn was poisoned by her beloved son Virgil."

13

CAYMAN ASKED BETTE, "YOU MUST HAVE BEEN bruiting this theory about for quite some time. Why are you so confident Virgil poisoned his mother?"

"Agatha and I discussed this when you were off doing other things. Since the curtain's been lifted on Mabel's affair with Ogden, let's try lifting a few other curtains. Nydia, I don't mean to offend you or open old wounds—"

"Too late!" snapped Nydia.

"So be it. If you intend not to be a sport about it, then I shall continue with a clear conscience. Although Mabel was whooping it up with Ogden, she thoroughly resented her lover's wife whooping it up with her favorite child."

Nydia jumped to her feet, raging. "That's absolute hogwash! Virgil and I didn't become interested in each other until after Ogden's death! I told you so myself."

"So . . . what?"

"It's the truth!" shouted Nydia.

"And I suppose the truth rises to the top, like cream in a bottle of milk." She looked at the others. "You do have bottled milk here, don't you?"

Agatha said with a smirk, "No, dear. We drink it directly from the udder."

"I'm sorry. I didn't mean to be condescending. But for English-speaking people, we're so terribly unalike!" She spun around and faced Nydia. "We have been spending a great deal of time together since we met on the ship, haven't we, Nydia?"

"Of course we have. What about it?"

"All things considered, we've gotten to know each other quite well."

"What are you getting at?"

"Nydia, you're a very strong woman. You're very determined. You have a sharp mind. You threw over a very promising stage career to marry into wealth even though the wealth belonged to a man with whom you were not in love."

"That's not so! I did love Ogden."

"If you insist. I think he bored you to the brink of desperation. You were an actress. In fact, in many ways you still are an actress. And actresses need excitement and stimulation and passion, oh, a hell of a lot of passion, unless you're Shirley Temple. Your first step in the direction of fulfillment came at the Houdini séance. Rama Singh, was that the medium's name?" Nydia nodded. "Ha! Now how'd I remember that one?"

"Because you made a point of remembering it," said Agatha.

"Sly puss. Rama Singh, Nydia. He detected the gift in you at his séance."

"Yes."

She said to Cayman, "Here's where I go deeper into trouble, but being a Yankee, I'm a very strong swimmer. Nydia, I am your friend, but I'll understand if you start hating me."

"I've started."

"Well, then, I think that before Rama Singh detected your gift, he detected a very unhappy and frustrated young lady who was ripe for a toss in the hay."

"Bitch!"

"And you tossed and it came up heads. Your sudden emergence as Rama Singh's protegée meant spending a lot of time with the Indian, and in time Ogden began suspecting the two of you were contacting each other as often as you were trying to contact the dead. Which led Ogden to encourage Mabel's case of the hots for him."

"Oh, God. Spare me." Sir Roland's hands were clasped together in supplication. Agatha wondered if he realized he might possibly have a climb to the gallows in his future.

" 'Hots.' That's an American expression, in case you haven't heard it before. So there were Nydia and Mr. Singh rolling around, I suppose on what they thought were magic carpets, and there were Mabel and Ogden tearing it off in a gazebo, of all unlikely places. Now then, I think Mabel was the sort of woman who wanted everything played in her favor."

"That's Mabel," said Agatha.

"Oh, Agatha," groaned Sir Roland.

"Really, Roland," said Agatha, who had less patience with hypocrisy than she did with murder. Murderers could be ingenious, but not hypocrites. "Don't waste a plea for pity on me. Reserve that for your judge and jury."

"May I continue?" asked Bette, lighting a cigarette. "After dumping Rama Singh or vice versa, or whatever, Nydia decided to set her cap for Virgil. Contrary to your remark that you thought Virgil was asexual, Nydia, I think you'd heard through the grapevine that Virgil was quite a jockey in the boudoir, a skill perfected by Virgil with liaisons on hot desert sands. I think I'd find bumping around on hot sand rather uncomfortable, but oh, what the hell."

"Bette, dear," said Agatha, "desert sands are quite cool at night."

"Why, thank you, Agatha. That is a comfort. I'll keep it in mind should I ever be offered a part in a film set in the Sahara. So, Nydia, you captivated Virgil, but unfortunately, once Mabel got wind of what was going on, she was having none of it. It was okay for her to be having it off with your husband, but you couldn't do likewise with her precious son. I won't go into the psychological aspects of Mabel's devotion to Virgil or vice versa, as I know I'm not qualified, but Mabel was as jealous as all get out. I think I'm right in assuming she told Virgil to chuck Nydia or he'd find himself written out of her will. That didn't sit too well with Virgil or with you either, Nydia." She took a dramatic pause. "Nydia, Agatha and I think Ogden's fortune wasn't all that large." Nydia said nothing. Agatha had visions of wheels of revenge twirling about in Nydia's head. "Although it was known that Mabel was dying, she wasn't dying soon enough. So Mabel had to go. And, my dear Inspector, so did Ogden."

Nydia was back on her feet shouting, "There are severe libel laws in this country! You'll find that out, Miss Bette Davis! Very severe libel laws!"

Bette's arms were flailing about and one hip jutted out, another Davis trademark. "Whatever the hell are you carrying on about? All I said was that Mabel had to go and so did Ogden."

"You have implied that Ogden did not die of natural causes! He died of a heart attack! Heart attack! Heart attack!"

"Cool it, girl," cautioned Bette, "or we'll soon be touching pinkies trying to contact you." She winked at Agatha and then turned to the inspector. He stood with Nayland, one on either side of Sir Roland, who sat with his face in his hands, quite disconsolate, and understandably so. Bette asked innocently, "Tell me, Nydia, what have I said to upset you so? Surely not the fact that Ogden had to go. You think I've implied murder. I could also have implied a divorce. But you must admit you did have need to be rid of him, and Virgil had to send Mabel off on her ultimate journey, and nobody's denying he didn't succeed. Am I wrong in surmising that Virgil didn't rat on his family's poison concerto dedicated to him because they knew he'd murdered Mabel and it was tit for tat, 'don't snitch on me and I don't snitch on you'? Though, mark my words, if I thought someone was poisoning me I'd soon tell Louella Parsons! Inspector, forgive me for stealing your thunder, but I had to say my piece."

"And quite a piece," said Cayman, restraining an urge to throw his arms around her and give her a genteel kiss on the lips.

"Bravo!" said Agatha. "I think it's time drinks were poured. Shall I be Mother?"

"Perfect casting," said Bette.

Cayman said to Nayland, "Lloyd, would you please escort Sir Roland to our car and take him back to Scotland Yard to be charged?"

"Inspector."

"Sir Roland?"

"My children. Anthea and Oscar. Theirs was not really a physical participation in killing Virgil. Those simple-minded ninnies simply went along with the plot because actually they had no choice."

"But they knew, didn't they?"

"Yes. They knew."

"And they did nothing to try and dissuade you?"

"No. There's nothing terribly original about them. Not in Oscar's music, not in Anthea's blank verse."

"Which Mabel at the séance threatened to recite and humiliate Anthea, though Anthea strongly insisted Mabel had never read any of her verse nor did Anthea ever read her any. I wonder, is there anything libelous in that?" asked Bette.

"I wouldn't think so," said Agatha. "Staying for the drink, Nydia? Roland, don't forget your hat and coat!"

"My hat and coat?" Bette wondered if he was genuinely confused or building up to a plea of insanity. "Ah, yes, my hat and coat."

"They're just here, sir," said Nayland, "lying on top of Mrs. Tilson's coat."

"Careful, Nayland," said Bette sotto voce in a swift aside. "There are strict libel laws in this country."

"Nydia," asked Agatha holding up the decanter of whisky, "are you joining us for another?"

"Why? Is there a shortage threatened?" Nydia was crossing to retrieve her coat.

Agatha said to no one in particular, "I do believe I detect a distinct chill in this room."

Nayland was guiding Sir Roland out of the room and into headlines, as across the room Nydia struggled into her coat, her face ashen. "It's understandable that I won't be here to catalogue the books tomorrow, Agatha. And of course I shall not be helping you settle in, Bette."

"Settle in! If I settled into this place after what's been going on, I'd be completely unsettled."

"My dear, dear Bette, I have a wonderful idea. My house is so large and commodious, and I really don't enjoy rambling about in it with no one to talk to but myself. Max will be away for ages, and even if he turns up unexpectedly, there's still plenty of room. I'd be so delighted if you accepted my hospitality and moved in with me."

Bette showed unsuppressed delight. "Agatha! How wonderful! You really want us to shack up together?"

Agatha looked nonplussed. " 'Shack up'? What is one doing when one is shacking up? Inspector, is it legal, whatever it is?"

Bette laughed. "You wonderful dodo. 'Shacking up' is an American expression and also an American pastime. In other words, 'to shack up' together is 'to live together.' "

Agatha expostulated with impatience, "I could never set a book in America! Never! 'Shack up'! 'Want some seafood, Mama?' I heard that one on shortwave. Come to think of it, I hear a lot of puzzling things on shortwave. Oh, well, that's neither here nor there. What do you say, Bette? Do we shack up together?"

"I'd be delighted," accepted Bette, "but I think Nydia disapproves of the idea. She's left us without so much as a fare-thee-well."

"Probably rushing home to rouse her solicitor."

194

"At this hour?" asked Cayman.

"I'm sure the sooner the better, as far as Nydia's concerned. Bette has put the fear of God into her. You're a very clever lady, Miss Bette Davis. You so carefully reasoned in your mind that Virgil killed Mabel, that Virgil and Nydia were having it off long before Ogden's death—"

"Come now, Agatha. Don't pussyfoot around with us. Nydia insisted on the séance. That's right. She didn't just suggest having one, she insisted. And the only persons she wanted to contact were the police. All that 'safety in numbers' jazz. Her impersonation of Mabel, and believe me that's just what it was. She can insist until she's blue in the face that we were actually hearing from Mabel. Nydia was disseminating suspicion, suspicion based on facts, because she was privy to them. She knew Virgil had killed Mabel because I think it was agreed between them that he would."

"Bette, you have no proof!" Cayman was a bit taken aback.

"Of course I have no proof. You have no proof. Agatha has no proof. Nydia was absolutely certain she was safe rushing in where angels fear to tread. She was safe because there was no possible way to prove she knew Virgil killed his mother and the rest of the family was killing him. As a matter of fact, if Sir Roland had had greater control over his terrible temper and kept that knife out of Virgil's mouth and Nellie's heart, he'd be on his way to his club for a nightcap instead of on his way to the pokey prodded by a nightstick."

"We do not prod with nightsticks. We use truncheons." Cayman was firm about that. "We're quite gentlemanly when running someone in, unless provoked. Then, to quote your James Cagney, 'I just might belt them one.'"

Agatha spoke up. "We're forgetting a minor character who must have made a major contribution."

"Someone else? You're making me feel terribly inadequate." Cayman drank more whisky. There was a lot of it in his glass, bless Agatha.

"Solomon Hubbard. The doctor. Doctor to the Tilsons and

the Wynns. It's reasonable to guess he signed Mabel and Ogden's death certificates. And if so, that could put him in shtook."

" 'Shtook'?" Bette was rightly puzzled. "Another ugly word."

"Between a rock and a hard place," explained Cayman. "In trouble. In hot water. Or how would you put it, Bette?"

"Up a certain creek without a paddle."

"We can set him aside until further notice," said Cayman. "To all intents and purposes, Mabel committed suicide and Ogden suffered a fatal heart attack. Hubbard probably had no reason to think otherwise."

"He's so far along in years," Agatha told them. "He should have retired ages ago."

"That's no excuse for falsifying death certificates," insisted Bette. "Please don't accuse me of overreacting, but I think the dear old man did as he was instructed. Probably with the promise of some healthy remuneration that would make his retirement sweet and comfortable. Am I being unkind to the elderly?"

"No, not at all," said Cayman. "You're being admirably logical. And I'm being deucedly slow. On the surface, this case is almost childishly simple. Below the surface, it boils and bubbles with all sorts of complications. I don't think proving Virgil might have murdered Mabel is any longer essential. They're both dead, so what's to be gained?"

"Setting the record straight," insisted Bette.

"Why?" asked Cayman.

"For someone who will undoubtedly one day write a book about this case."

"Yes, yes," said Agatha with a sigh. "It is inevitable."

"Agatha, why don't you write the book?" Bette was serious.

"Maybe someday it will be tempting, but right now I prefer to stick to fiction. I'd rather manipulate than be manipulated. Now, Bette." She was off on a new tack. "About your trial. Would it bother you if I attended every day?"

"Why, Agatha, I'd be delighted! You'll be giving me moral support!"

"For ages now I've been thinking of writing a play set in a courtroom. The Old Bailey, of course. I need to brush up on courtroom procedures and deportment and etiquette. Do you think yours is going to be a bit of a messy case?"

"No more messy than anything involving the Warner brothers."

"I'm sure I can depend on you to spice it up a bit," said Agatha. She looked at her wristwatch. "Oh, dear! I'm for bed. Look at the time! I'm sure I'm exhausted. But first, Bette, I shall prepare your room."

"Do it in the morning, darling. I'll spend the night here. It's much too late to start moving things."

"Aren't you afraid you might hear digging noises?" asked Agatha.

"There won't be digging noises until tomorrow morning, when my men are scheduled to show up. And—" Cayman was staring past Agatha and Bette. The women turned and saw Anthea standing in the doorway.

"I let myself in with my key. I always let myself in with my key. Virgil wants me to have a key because he enjoys my company. There's no constable guarding the gate. There's no one guarding the gate."

"There's no need," said Cayman. "I'm here."

She loosened the head shawl tied at her neck. "It's begun to rain. It's really a very fine mist. I've been walking a very long time."

"Please sit down," invited Bette as she looked from Cayman to Agatha and back to Anthea. "Would you like some port? Some sherry?"

Anthea sat in a straight-backed chair. "I was looking for Father. Isn't he here?"

"He's at Scotland Yard," Cayman told her.

"Why? What's he doing there?"

Cayman felt uncomfortable. Anthea was supposed to be at

home attended to by her brother while she had hysterics. She was far from hysterical now. "Sir Roland has been taken into custody."

"Why?" Bette moved closer to Agatha. Anthea had put her in mind of Ophelia slowly going mad, but there was no pond in the garden for Ophelia to drown herself in.

Agatha took command. "Wasn't Oscar with you? Where is he?"

"He's asleep on my bed. His throat's been cut."

The sharp intake of breath was Bette's.

Cayman asked, "Who cut his throat? Did he commit suicide?"

She said slowly, "It takes courage to commit suicide. That's why I'm still alive. I need to be with Father. I need him to comfort me. There's no one to comfort me. Virgil's gone. And Oscar was mean to me. He said he'd testify against me. He said the Crown would sentence me to hang." She cackled. Bette assumed she thought she was laughing. "Where's Nellie? Why isn't she here?" She shouted, "Nellie! Nellie! Bring me a cup of tea! I'm cold. I'm very, very cold." She folded her hands and laid them in her lap. "Oscar was so surprised when I leapt at him with the knife. It's the first time I've ever taken Oscar by surprise." She thought for a moment. "I've never taken anyone by surprise."

"Oh, yes you have, my dear. There are three more you've taken by surprise."

Anthea sighed heavily. "We are such a wicked family. But she's far more wicked than we are."

Bette's adrenaline was at a boil. Agatha controlled her excitement by pouring herself another whisky.

Calmly Cayman asked, "Who's far more wicked?"

Anthea lost patience. "Oh, don't be such a ninny! Nydia, of course! Who else but Nydia? She's always scheming. Mother was the first to recognize that. Mother knew Ogden had weaseled his way into her heart to get some of her money, and she didn't mind one bit. But when she saw Nydia setting her cap for Virgil, well, that was too much. Virgil told me Nydia poisoned Ogden. He knew I'd tell no one. I'm only telling you now because there's only Father, Nellie, and myself to take the blame with Nydia." She made fists and pounded her lap. "She'll get away scot free! I bet you she'll get away scot free! Please! Somebody! Please fetch Mamby!"

Cayman phoned the Yard for Nayland to return with a detective and a matron, while Agatha told Anthea that Mamby had gone to her sister, who had been taken suddenly ill.

"Suddenly ill? Ha ha ha ha ha! Suddenly ill? Why should Mamby want to poison her sister?" She dissolved into uncontrollable weeping.

It was that rare occasion when Bette's hands were trembling. She was having difficulty lighting a cigarette. Cayman rescued the lighter from her hand, and in seconds Bette was enjoying a heavy drag on the cigarette. "Well, hasn't this been quite a day! Wait until I tell Ruthie!" She watched Agatha trying to control and comfort Anthea. The weeping was giving way to hysteria, and Agatha was sure that Anthea would soon be in the kind of state that would make her testimony useless to the Crown. She expressed her doubts to Cayman, who nodded his head in agreement.

Bette said to Agatha, "I was right on the nose, wasn't I? I really figured the whole damned thing out." She took another puff. "And unless I get notarized proof from the two of you, nobody in Hollywood will believe me! Oh, God, why are so many people so mean to each other?"

Agatha didn't try to answer that one, because it would have taken the rest of the night. Instead, she asked Cayman, "I didn't hear you ordering Nydia picked up and brought in."

"On the testimony of Anthea Wynn? You want me to be a laughingstock?"

"You mean Nydia gets away with it?" Bette was shocked and angry.

"Time will tell, Bette. Time will tell."

Agatha held Anthea close to her. "You poor dear. Soon you'll be in a nice little haven where you can paper the blank walls with specimens of your blank verse. And as to Nydia Tilson, my money's on her troubled conscience. She'll have her comeuppance from that." She looked at Cayman and Bette. "Don't you agree?"

Bette looked both regal and noble as she said, "I think another quote from Shakespeare is very apt for Nydia. 'Leave her to heaven.' " She said to Cayman with a beguiling smile, "Inspector, can I entice you to stay for breakfast?"

He was easily enticed. He was very hungry.